VIDEO VIXEN

*Also by Elaine Raco Chase
in Large Print:*

Calculated Risk
Special Delivery

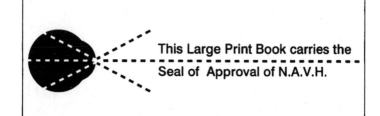

This Large Print Book carries the
Seal of Approval of N.A.V.H.

VIDEO VIXEN

Elaine Raco Chase

Thorndike Press • Thorndike, Maine

Published in 2000 by arrangement with Writers House
Publishers.

Thorndike Press Large Print ® Romance Series.

The tree indicium is a trademark of Thorndike Press.

The text of this Large Print edition is unabridged.
Other aspects of the book may vary from the original edition.

Set in 16 pt. Plantin.

Printed in the United States on permanent paper.

Library of Congress Cataloging-in-Publication Data

Chase, Elaine Raco, 1949–
    Video vixen / Elaine Raco Chase.
      p. cm.
    ISBN 0-7862-2490-8 (lg. print : hc : alk. paper)
    1. Television actors and actresses — Fiction. 2. Large
type books. I. Title.
    PS3553.H3333 V53   2000
    813'.54—dc21   00-021591

VIDEO VIXEN

CHAPTER ONE

The three main topics of conversation among the luncheon crowd in Maxwell's Plum were the current price of gold, Wall Street's noontime rally, and yesterday's fifteen inches of snow that paralyzed Manhattan, closing both LaGuardia and Kennedy airports. Of course all that changed when *she* walked in wearing the now notorious coat.

The fur was mink — boot-length, double-breasted, and cut like a man's jacket. Luxurious black pelts, lined in *her* shade of scarlet silk, that rippled and flowed over the well-proportioned woman cocooned inside. The wide shawl collar and oversized black mink beret framed an equally notorious face.

Elbows nudged elbows, gazes left their windowed study of snowplow architecture, E. F. Hutton's advice ceased to be bantered against Merrill Lynch's. The famed restaurant's excellent cuisine was abandoned. Appetites were piqued but not by the food. Hungry patrons let their eyes feast on an infinitely more interesting entrée.

Jerry Corry was the only man in the room not watching *her*. And why should he? He knew *her* intimately, from the long, luxuriously wavy chestnut hair with its distinctive widow's peak, the high, smooth forehead, the straight nose, crystal-clear blue eyes that pierced a man's soul, full lips, and slightly square jaw all sitting atop a full-breasted yet supple five foot seven inch frame.

With his shoulders relaxed against the leather-backed chair, Jerry viewed the approaching diner's reactions with supreme satisfaction. When she stopped at his table, he rose, kissed her on one winter-flushed cheek, and heard a chorus of envious masculine sighs.

"I know you don't have much time, so I took the liberty of ordering: French onion soup, salad niçoise, and limed mineral water." He watched as the mink was shrugged off, revealing a black knit dress with a vivid red Chanel jacket. His brown gaze shifted to study her face. "You look tired."

One precisely defined eyebrow arched and a smile lifted the corners of scandalously scarlet lips. "I did have an exhausting morning." Her throaty voice purred a subliminal message. "I seduced my virginal eighteen-year-old stepson in the hot tub while my crippled husband played grateful voyeur. Then I posed for a revealing fashion layout. Now I'll take care of you and later" — thick black velvet lashes lowered demurley — "I'm scheduled to ravish the local minister who has been making quite a nuisance of himself."

Laughter and a pleased expression etched Jerry Corry's angular face. "Victoria Kirkland, at last you are enjoying the role of Vixen Mallory!"

"You're giving me no choice!" came her tart rejoinder. Vikki leaned forward; one scarlet-coated fingernail tapped the crystal on his gold watch. "Hundreds of eyes are boring into my back this very minute. Hopefully they're all talking about the billboard featuring this mink coat that was unveiled in Times Square yesterday."

"Hopefully they are discussing more than that gorgeous gigantic ad and the stunning woman in the mink," Jerry corrected her. "Hopefully they are discussing what sixteen million other Americans talk about every day. The program that has made twelve thirty to one thirty *the* lunch hour for businesses, home-

9

makers, and college students.

"I'm betting my job as PR man on the fact that everyone in this restaurant is whispering about *Always Tomorrow*, Garner Broadcasting's cable-TV entry into the daytime soaps and currently number one in the ratings against all the major networks combined."

"Number one!" Vikki's kohl-rimmed eyes widened. "I — I hadn't realized the rating books had come out."

A Cheshire-cat grin spread Jerry's mouth; his arms crossed complacently over his chest. "I'm going to tell the entire cast and crew later this evening after the final taping. Only eighteen months on the air and, courtesy of a super satellite, number one in the country!"

Conversation was halted when the bow-tied waiter brought their luncheon order. The young man's hand noticeably shook when he placed the steaming liquid appetizer and salad in front of Vikki. The waiter continued to hover, straightening unused silverware, adding water to untouched ice-filled goblets, dusting nearly invisible crumbs from the pristine white cloth until a superior's peremptory voice hailed him.

Jerry's grin broadened even further; his hand smoothed graying blond hair that

10

grew thick despite an ever-receding hair-
line. "I love it!"

Vikki looked up, her spoon continuing to
pierce the tight seal of mozzarella cheese
that blanketed the savory onion broth.
"Love what?"

"You still don't take it in, do you?" At
her bewildered expression Jerry exhaled a
patient sigh. "You, Victoria Kirkland, are
lusted after by ninety percent of the male
population. According to *TV Guide*, various soap magazines and a small notation
in *Time*, you are currently the most scheming, manipulative woman on TV, who is
seldom found in anything but a horizontal
position and whose torrid, uncensored
cable love scenes make regular network
officials pale and envious."

"You're describing Vixen Mallory, Jerry,"
Vikki countered. "She's the one who has
been married four times, murdered her last
two husbands and was never caught, had
three abortions, has been raped, kidnapped, and enslaved, seduced her stepson
and minister, succeeded in driving her
sister-in-law insane . . ." She drew a deep,
chastising breath. "You had the nerve to
say I looked tired!"

Their joint laughter caused the sur-
rounding patrons' heads to turn. Again

11

Vikki fell victim to whispers and questionable glances. Shifting in nervous discomfort, she reached for a calming mouthful of mineral water.

"All humility aside" — Jerry paused to blow across the spoonful of steaming soup — "this plan of mine has worked out brilliantly. I've kept the entire cast, writers, and crew in a cloak of mystery for the last year and a half, letting the news media's imagination run wild with titillating stories leaked here and there. Fans are chomping at the proverbial bit to read, see, and hear anything about *Always Tomorrow.*"

He rubbed his hands together in a savoring gesture. "Vikki, this is going to be *the* year." Jerry's index finger stabbed the air. "*Your* year. Do you know your fan mail has jumped to five thousand letters a week!"

"I'm afraid to ask how many are death threats."

"None! Vikki" — he twisted the gold nugget ring on his pinky — "the women of America admire your strength, your spirit. Vixen Mallory goes after what she wants. Nothing and no one gets in her way. She spits at sentimentality." Jerry's expression was serious. "While the men may lust and fantasize about being seduced by Vixen,

12

women fantasize too. They want to be Vixen. They're tired of being victims; they want to stir things up and take what they want without a twinge of conscience."

Vikki opened her mouth but once again the public relations man's voice interrupted. "Vixen Mallory is going to be number one this year. The billboard and the mink ads are just a warning. This hits the newsstands today." Jerry handed her the January issue of *Playboy*. "The layout is bright, witty, and tasteful. Peter Finch's camera lens loves you. He's going to be the photographer on next week's Vixen perfume ads."

Blue eyes briefly inspected the glossy pages of the fabled men's magazine. Vikki silently wondered how her parents would take to this latest publicity gimmick. Maybe the magazine wasn't sold aboard the cruise ship they were on in the South Pacific. "This will definitely cause a commotion." She drew a deep breath.

"It had better or I'm out of a job!" With a satisfied smile, Jerry spread chocolate butter on warm, fresh bread. "You know, Vikki, you've been one helluva good sport about doing all this." He shook his head. "I remember the all-night session the cast and I had talking you into being the show's main focus."

She stared at the salad, her fork spearing a vinaigrette-glossed potato and anchovy. "I'd do anything for them. They're top-rate professionals, all of them. Besides being twenty of the most wonderful human beings I have ever met." Vikki's eyes locked into Jerry's. "We are a family, working eighteen to twenty hours a day on a labor of love.

"We both know Vixen Mallory was a fluke, an accident. I was the associate producer on an up-and-coming cable soap and one day an extra didn't show. I just happened to have a union card and could fit into the slinky dress that was in the wardrobe department. I knew nothing about acting."

Jerry swallowed a mouthful of lettuce. "As I recall, all you did was sit in a chair, cross those long legs, and begin to unbutton the dress." One brown eye gave a broad wink. "Face it, Vikki, you're a natural talent." He tapped the cover of *Playboy*. "You photograph beautifully. You convey more with those wicked blue eyes and pouty lips than an army of trained professionals."

Vikki stared at the magazine for a long time, a myriad of memories clicking

14

through her mind. Suddenly a very vixenish laugh bubbled from her throat. "I'd
love to get my hands on two hundred and
twelve issues."

"Well, I — I suppose." He blotted his
lips. "I know you have a big family but . . ."

"Not family, Jerry. That's how many kids
were in my high school graduating class."
At his baffled expression she continued.
"Let's be brutally honest for a moment.
Without the designer wardrobe I've been
fitted into and allowed to use, without the
considerable talents of the studio makeup
man and hairdresser, precision lighting,
and practiced camera angles, I'm just a
plain Jane."

Her upraised palm halted his sputtered
interruption. "You are promoting a girl
who was twenty pounds overweight all
through high school and college, who kept
Clearasil in business and nearly developed
curvature of the spine from trying to hide
breasts that developed in the fifth grade."
Vikki's lips twisted against remembered
adolescent cruelties.

"In the sixties all the girls emulated that
English fashion model Twiggy. Well, I was
neither flat nor curl-free." Her long fingers
pulled against the cascade of hair that tumbled against her shoulders. "My father

15

came home early from work and caught me ironing my hair. I can still feel that beating! My brothers claim they don't recognize me without the giant purple rollers I wore twenty hours a day trying to straighten out this Shirley Temple mop.

"I never had a date all through high school. I missed the junior prom and the boy I asked to the senior ball turned me down. College, well . . ." She licked full lips. "That was all work and no play until I met Gregg. He saw the woman that had been hiding in me; he goaded, teased, nurtured, and loved me, but then" — her voice faltered — "he was taken away."

Vikki's chin tilted downward, her gaze concentrated on the magazine. "I'd dearly love to send two hundred and twelve issues out with a big: *So there!* scrawled on each cover!"

Long scarlet-tipped fingers curved around her glass, lifting in a toasting gesture. "Here's to a dynamite year for you, continued number-one status for *Always Tomorrow* and" — Vikki favored Jerry with a wide-eyed glance and disarming smile — "here's to Video Vixen, the lady who's given me the best year of my life and who made turning thirty a prime number!" Their glasses clicked to a simultaneous "amen."

"I am very glad your attitude has changed, Vikki. You were a little . . . um . . . pigheaded about accepting any of these fashion layouts and the cosmetic contract."

"Awed and overwhelmed," she rectified. "It's a new experience for me to be wanted for my . . . body."

Jerry aimed a butter-smeared knife at her. "You really are a natural in front of any camera. Stick with me, kid, and you'll have fame and fortune."

Her empty soup bowl was pushed to one side. "The fortune part is heavenly. I'm making more in one day than I ever did in a week. I'm also enjoying giving back to my parents a little fun they so richly deserve. But the fame" — Vikki's eyebrows arched — "I'm a realist. Fame is fleeting. I'll have some fun." She gave a low laugh. "Those phantom writers in their Mt. Olympus office towers may decide to" — her index finger sliced across her throat — "eliminate the scheming villainess."

"Not unless your fan mail drops below five hundred letters a week," came his dry quip. "Seriously, Vik, on screen or off, you handle yourself like a pro. The hierarchy loves the fad that Vixen Mallory is no vacuous cupcake."

Her fork toyed with a black olive, batting

it back and forth across the nearly empty salad plate. "They have the real *stars* to thank for that. Turning Vikki into Vixen took the combined talents of everyone involved. It took a lot of perseverance to teach this rank amateur about voice inflection, movement, presence, and hundreds of other essentials." Vikki exhaled a trapped breath. "I'm smart enough to realize this is just an event in my life, not a career, and when all this melts, I'm lucky enough to have a master's degree in broadcasting to fall back on."

A gold napkin wiped thin lips. "Nothing is going to melt" — Jerry nodded toward Maxwell's Plum full wall of ice-crystal-etched windows — "especially in this rotten January weather. I've got a few plans to map out for the next onslaught of publicity. How would you feel about flying to Chicago to let Phil Donahue take a crack at an hour with Vixen?"

"I noticed you said *Vixen* not Vikki."

"Image, baby, image. You think the public is going to want to hear that you live in a converted carriage house in Connecticut, like to do needlepoint and crewel, put up fresh jam, and bake bread?" Jerry's tone issued a stern warning.

"Being Victoria Kirkland anyplace but in

18

the safety and confines of your own hon is the kiss of death. No one wants to hear how 'nice' you are. That you have great parents, four terrific brothers, love fox terriers, and work at the local level for stiffer drunk-driving laws."

"But . . . but . . . Jerry!" she sputtered in abject alarm. "That is me. Vikki is real. Vixen is not."

"But . . . but . . ." he mimicked, "the fans don't put a great deal of distance between the actress and the character. They expect you to *be* Vixen. Expect, hell! They demand it."

Elbows on the table, Jerry's voice lost its biting edge. "Let me share a few facts with you, Vikki. Soap operas were once mere fillers. They now are the number-one form of TV entertainment, pulling in over sixty-six percent of network income. There are magazines devoted to shows and stars. Fifty-five percent of the audience may be housewives, but soap fever bubbles in big-city bars, office buildings, and on college campuses.

"Today soap opera is no longer a denigrating, cliché term. Soaps are well-written and carefully conceived to make people aware of a variety of problems, and how and where to get help and cope with those ns. Characters and story lines ne extended families to viewers. ults develop." Jerry's brown eyes narrowed.

"Those cults are for Vixen Mallory, not Vikki Kirkland. Vixen's the character they connect with, cheer at, cry with, swear at, hate, and love. Vixen's *it*. The fans live vicariously through her. Preserve Vixen. Shield her. Don't let anyone or anything destroy her."

A shiver coursed Vikki's spine despite the opulent warmth provided by the black mink. "I guess this Vixen's a virgin when it comes to knowing the public's reaction. I just assumed everyone realizes that the characters in *Always Tomorrow* are pure celluloid. Now I'm scared."

"Good." He relaxed against the leather-backed dining chair, opening the single button of his charcoal suit jacket. "I want you to be on guard twenty-four hours a day. You are a hot ticket that I intend to keep at the boiling point."

Playing Vixen Mallory during nonworking hours was going to require a more intense acting talent, Vikki rationalized with silent contemplation. As it was, her soap role consumed eighteen to twenty hours a day; adding in the newly acquired cosmetic contract, upcoming interviews, and personal appearances, Victoria Kirkland would disappear. Would that be so harmful?

That dealer of deleterious deeds, Vixen, had propelled Vikki further than she had ever dreamed. Why not sit back and relax and let that vivid, vital vamp reap a few rewards? At least for a while.

After examining the check, Jerry ripped off the receipt and tossed a collection of bills on the table. "Why don't we share a cab? I'll drop you off at the Fifty-sixth Street studio before I head over to my office. I've got a few irons in the fire that need a gourmet's touch. I'll be in to talk to the cast and writers after the final taping, around nine tonight."

He took temporary possession of the fur coat, holding the bulk of the weight as Vikki's arms slid into the red-silk-lined sleeves. His hands brought the wide collar up around her face. "Goodness, you and this mink make a stunning pair."

Cosmetic wizardry turned ice-blue eyes into exotic slits that formed the now famous vixen glance. "*Goodness* had little to do with it!"

Her tart, coquettish voice turned serious against his laughter. "Although I wouldn't have done the ad or taken the coat without prior assurance that these animals were bred for consumer use."

Jerry gave an understanding nod. "Vikki needed the assurance; Vixen would have preferred the minks be on the endangered species list."

With a masculine hand pressed against the small of her back, Vikki wended her way through the occupied tables. She courteously tried to avoid dragging the sumptuous fur against any of the seated diners. Her successful exit was dramatically halted when a rude, bulging-veined hand sank into the soft, thick lustrous mink.

"Look, Harriet! See! I told you it was *her!*" Fingers still gripping the fur hem, a short, rather barrel-figured woman stood up. "It is *you*, isn't it?"

With a mixture of surprise and fear Vikki viewed a freckled face framed by excessively short brassy blond hair. She tried to free the coat and, failing, stepped back against Jerry's protective bulk. "Excuse me. I — I —"

"Don't deny it!" The nasal voice grew louder, much to the delight of the interested bystanders. "I know you and your husband and your lover." Prying eyes inspected Jerry, noticing his wedding band. The tone grew triumphant. "Is this your next victim, you scheming hussy? How could you ruin so many lives without even a thought?" A warning finger was pushed into Vikki's face. "You can't keep getting away with this! That wonderful Reverend Patrick Malone knows what you did to your last husband. He's not going to let you get away with murdering anyone else."

"Betty's right," added the woman named Harriet, her voice as tight as the gray curls that framed an angular face. Brown eyes stared into Vikki's stupefied expression. "You are evil! I know what you're trying to do to your sweet sister-in-law, that trusting angel of a girl. You're trying to drive her insane. She's so confused." The words caught in her throat, she sniffed and wiped her nose against her napkin. "Betty, let go of that coat. No telling *where* it's been." A shudder twitched thin shoulders.

Jerry's whispered "Careful, *Vixen*" vibrated in Vikki's ear. Ten elegant fingers moved sinuously up the wide lapels on the mink to adjust the shawl collar. "My sister-in-law is a simpering wimp," came her throaty response. "Beth has difficulty putting a straight part in that Alice-in-

Wonderland blond hair of hers. I'm trying to help the girl; point out her weaknesses."

Her seductive voice continued. "And *wonderful* Reverend Malone?" Vikki's face turned slightly to the left, chin tipped downward, dark lashes narrowed over clear blue eyes. "I don't suppose you notice how the good Reverend enjoys more than his share of his afternoon sherry. And isn't he the eavesdropper?" The two women exchanged meaningful glances. "I'll tell you what else the good reverend enjoys." Vikki leaned close to the woman's ear and whispered.

"Black lace *what?*" Betty gasped, released her hold on the fur, and fell back into her chair.

"What? What!" The words squeaked from Harriet's throat as she watched Betty fan herself with her hand.

Betty's strangled tone rose above her companion's. "Wh-when?" She demanded from Vikki.

"Tomorrow."

"We'll cancel those tickets to that Broadway show," she told Harriet. "We'll call the girls back home. You won't believe what she just told me!" Betty gave Vikki her sweetest smile. "All thirty-two members of our garden club watch you every

24

day. Could you . . . please autograph" — her stubby fingers rummaged through her purse — "this?"

"Your parking voucher?"

"No . . . oh, dear they'll want that, won't they? Harriet!"

"Here, Miss Mallory." The other, less-flustered woman supplied a hastily ripped sheet of paper. "Just say something won-derfully wicked to Harriet and Betty from Schenectady."

Using Jerry's felt-tipped pen, Vikki signed the requested note with unprece-dented flourish. "How's that, ladies?"

Harriet made a quick grab, read the inscription, and, smiling, passed it to her companion. "I love your clothes. Where did you get that tiny red and black sheer teddy you had on yesterday? Wouldn't Gordon just love me in that, Betty?"

Jerry supplied the answer. "Saks Fifth Avenue." He gently pushed Vikki toward the glass-etched front door. "They're set-ting up a Vixen lingerie display tomorrow. All in scarlet and black, of course." The two women oohed and aahed over that information, then went on to discuss the possibility that wonderful Reverend Ma-lone was possibly only posing as a min-ister.

"You were brilliant." The PR man gave Vikki a complimentary hug.

"A Vixen lingerie display?" she inquired once they were on the snow-edged sidewalk. "Now that's spur-of-the-moment brilliance!"

Jerry whistled for a cab. "I spoke the truth," he protested with studied innocence. "Just another one of my genius suggestions. Since Saks is providing part of the wardrobe on the show, they jumped at the tie-in." He frowned at the bustling traffic. "Why don't you try hailing the cab?"

Her melodic laughter formed wispy puffs in the dry frigid air. "You think Vixen will have better luck?" Vikki shook her head. "New York cabbies are immune. They're used to Jackie O, Cher, Barbara Walters, Lauren Bacall, and Hepburn. I waited for over ten minutes just trying to get one to take me here."

Stepping off the curb and well into the street, Jerry called back. "Look at the way those two ladies reacted. The fans want Vixen." Two more sharp whistles pierced the air, but the cabs continued whizzing past. "Come on, Miss *Mallory*, give it a try.

Lifting her face from the mink's protection, she moved to Jerry's side and extended one black-leather-gloved hand in a regal, imperious gesture. Within seconds a cab came speeding to a halt. Vikki was impressed. "If the fans want Vixen" — she yanked open the door — "then Vixen they'll get!" Her good-natured wink said it all!

CHAPTER TWO

"Close the door, Hallen, or do you want the whole department to hear what a stupid, incompetent SOB you really are!"

The glass door swung shut. "Now, Dan, wait just one minute. Don't ream my a—"

Daniel Falkner pushed his imposing six-foot, broad-shouldered frame off the brown tweed executive chair. "Shut up and sit down." Brown eyes dissected his subordinate's small frame and bushy red hair. "You call yourself a newsman? Hell, I don't know what made Haskell hire the likes of you."

Lungs inhaling a deep, steadying breath, Dan settled back behind his desk. "The powers that be have spent the last hour giving me a verbal lashing that rightly belongs to you and Haskell." A fist formed around this week's issue of *Newsmaker* magazine, sending the slick spiraling toward the pale-complexioned reporter. "This piece of consummate *crap* may cost us a lawsuit, and that's if we're lucky."

"There's not one libelous statement in

there," Kip declared, rummaging in the breast pocket of his plaid shirt for a cigarette. "I was assigned to do an in-depth report on the major networks' daytime programing. That's my first piece." Four twisted paper matches were discarded before he was finally able to light up. The nicotine fueled Kip's confidence. "No one complained or *edited* last week's overview."

Dan was thoughtful for a moment. "Your cover story was basically a list of media statistics, ratings, and advertising focal points," came his qualified reminder. "This . . . story" — he swallowed the sour taste in his mouth — "was hardly that."

"I can back every statement." The cigarette jabbed the air, sending gray ashes falling on the brown carpet. "I — I've got all my cassette tapes and notes."

"Cassette tapes and notes!" Dan's normally deep voice rose an octave to match his squeaky companion's. "I'm sure you have them and I bet they'll say exactly what you want them to." A dangerous smile creased his rough-hewn features. "What you did, Hallen, was transport yourself back in time and you thought you were still at that supermarket rag, the *Global Tatler*. Need I remind you that little gem suffered one lawsuit too many and went under.

"When you're writing a *Newsmaker* piece you don't play God, you don't judge. You research, provide information both pro and con, and let the reader decide." Dan pulled another issue of the magazine from his red In basket. "You took quotes out of context, added innuendos, and suppositions, and your quote reliable source unquote turned out to be a fired extra that was trying to get back at the network and their top rated show."

Kip shifted his boxy weight in discomfort and reached for another tobacco crutch. "Now, just listen to me. Please, Dan . . ." When his dark gaze focused on the anger that etched his boss's eyes and face, he cleared his throat and tried a more ingratiating approach. "I spent two very intense weeks at that network, studying and working on all four of their shows from the lowest rated to the top. I interviewed all the major *stars*" — Kip had difficulty not sneering that last word — "writers, and producers. That's how I set my tone."

"Well, your *tone* stinks, Hallen." Dan's blunt forefinger punctured the explanation. "Upstairs received enough angry calls today that the switchboard blew a transformer." His satanic smile returned. "The readers are livid. You defamed characters and shows they love. The network in question just pulled all their magazine advertising and the cast, crew, and writers are talking with their lawyers."

"How . . . how about an apology?" Kip stuttered the offer.

"How about you giving me the rest of your files on the other networks before you leave on an indefinite suspension."

"You can't do that!" The reporter jumped to his sneaker-clad feet. "I've got a two-year contract. I've got . . ."

"You've got fine print; I suggest you take the next six weeks to read it," Dan intervened in a low, authoritative voice. "During your hiatus I recommend you enroll in an accredited institute of higher learning." He nodded toward the door. "Bring in your material, then get out."

Two minutes later a somber, jean-clad figure gingerly deposited three burgeoning file folders on the center of Dan's walnut-grained desk. Dan failed to notice; his dark gaze was concentrated on the serenely falling snowflakes that swirled past his tenth-floor office window.

For the first time in the two years since

he became assignments editor at *Newsmaker*, Dan wished he were back overseas. Doing TV news reports from a helicopter over the DMZ, hiding from marauding guerrillas in El Salvador, or running through the rubble that was Lebanon had never elevated his blood pressure the way Kip Hallen had.

One weary palm tried to massage the tension from his neck. He didn't doubt another gray strand had been added to his thick head of hair. Dan silently cursed Ryan Haskell, his counterpart on the magazine's feature section, for being on a two-week Caribbean holiday. Hallen was a problem he hadn't expected to inherit. Correcting that problem was going to disrupt a lot of schedules.

Dan swung his chair around and reached for his phone. "Gary? Will you and Paul come in here please?"

He looked at two of the magazine's most competent field reporters. "Look, I hate to yank you guys off that EPA story, but that's not scheduled till March and I've got a more presssing problem." He tapped the cover of the latest issue. "You can read Hallen's mistake, but I don't want to read yours in the next two *Newsmakers*."

Gary Dale pushed the nosepiece of his

pewter-framed glasses against his face. "You mean that daytime time soap piece?" His dark gaze shifted to his partner, Paul Wyatt. "How in hell could he screw up that bit of fluff?"

"The same way he screwed up the opera story he did last month," Paul intoned, looking at Dan. "I happened to be at Haskell's desk the day the Met called and screamed — fortissimo," came his wry rejoiner.

Dan emitted a low groan, looking from one, man to the other. "Had I known that, I would have made Hallen's suspension a firing. Damn, when Ryan gets back he can clean out his own house." A warning gaze was directed. "Don't give me cause to clean out mine." He picked up the file folders. "I don't know what you're going to find in here. The articles were to focus on the daytime soap phenomenon, each network getting evaluated, pro and con, interviews with cast, crew, writers, and major advertisers. See if you can't get some viewer reaction."

Dan handed them each a folder and was dismayed to find one extra. "Hell, I don't have anyone free to do the cable show."

"*Always Tomorrow?*" Paul Wyatt's blond brows arched with interest. "I'll swap."

"Wait a minute." Gary's arm brushed aside the other man's outstretched hand. "I'll be glad to take it."

"Whoa," Dan's fist held the file down on the desk. "What's up? What's the attraction?"

"Vixen Mallory," was the answer they both gave without hesitation. Paul looked at Gary and they both laughed. "Is that why you've been taking your lunch at twelve-thirty?" Paul inquired.

Gary gave a sheepish grin. "I got hooked when I went into the hospital two months back for that hernia operation. All of St. Mary's stopped for the hour. Heaven help you if you rang your buzzer! How about you?"

Paul picked a thread off his rolled blue shirtsleeve. "I started watching over at McClory's, where I have lunch. Ed put in one of those six-foot screens for the sports crowd, but the soap crowd proved a bigger draw. Six feet of Vixen Mallory," he sighed. "Delicious! Did you see the Times Square billboard?"

"Did you get this month's *Playboy*?" At his partner's negative response, Gary grinned. "Five of the most gorgeous, glossy pages of Vixen."

"I can't believe you two guys are hung

34

up over a soap opera character." Dan shook his gray head in disbelief.

Gary winked at his partner. "You'll have to make sure you read our articles. My wife has been watching soaps for years and I always teased her about them until I was laid up. The shows are extremely well written; the actors and actresses do a remarkable job. Don't forget they are on *every* day, not just once a week."

"How creative can they get in a kitchen?"

"I don't think *Always Tomorrow* has a kitchen," Paul returned with a broad smile. "Lots of bedrooms. Did you see Vixen in that black nightgown last Tuesday? The back dropped right off the TV screen. I never thought a spine could look so good. I'm getting Marlene one for Valentine's Day."

Gary rubbed his jaw for a thoughtful moment. "Dan, I'll treat you to a month of dinners anywhere if I can take *Always Tomorrow*."

"I've got season tickets to the Garden," Paul countered that offer. "They're yours."

Dan's brown eyes swung from one eager face to the other, then down to his desk. Interested fingers opened the red-labeled folder and stroked through various printed material until they found a series of color glossies provided by the studio's public relations department.

Guileless blue eyes stared up from the photograph, an arresting face framed by a froth of dark curls and a provocative ruby smile. "I think I'll take *Always Tomorrow* for myself," came Dan's sudden decision.

"Spoil sport!" Paul grinned and nudged his partner. "Gary, I think our boss has been Vixenized."

"Hey, didn't I just mention how tight schedules were around here?" Dan protested with an easy smile. "This will be the last article in the series; I'll have two weeks to work on it between my regular desk duties." He found it impossible to keep his gaze off the picture. "I won't deny you've whetted my appetite."

"For the show or Vixen Mallory?" bantered a disappointed Gary.

A grin formed on Dan's mouth. "Which do you think?"

"Vikki, these apple and cheese croissants are absolutely delicious." That verbal sentiment was echoed by other cast members on *Always Tomorrow* as they lounged on the struck sound stage.

A shy smiled etched her well-scrubbed

features. Vikki took a relaxing sip of mulled cider and tried to wiggle into a comfortable position on the set's sofa. The massive white conversation pit felt exactly like what it didn't appear to be — a rock. The thinly cushioned particle board provided little comfort to her gray jogging-suit-covered form.

"When did you find time to make these?" inquired David Cushing, the actor who portrayed Reverend Malone.

"While you were straightening a very crooked collar." Vikki parried with an amused wink. Her comment brought forth a chorus of chuckles.

She looked at the studio clock and frowned. "I can't imagine what's keeping Jerry. He should have been here half an hour ago." Only four of her castmates and one writer had stayed past the final taping. The others, fearing the strength of another winter storm, had headed for home.

"I'll eat his share." David boldly confiscated the last golden-crusted pastry. "By the way, your billboard looks fantastic. You're causing quite a traffic jam in Times Square. People are looking up instead of at the lights."

Vikki watched her toes wiggle inside her bright red slipper-socks. "It certainly fills the sky," she agreed on a wry note. "I remember when I was a kid, seeing that smoking billboard of John Wayne in that spot. Never in my wildest dreams did I ever expect to replace the Duke!"

"You look marvelous," agreed Heather Stuart, who played Vixen's sister-in-law, Beth. "And that coat! Is it really yours to keep?" Her blond eyebrows arched in interested speculation.

"In lieu of a modeling fee and making me a perpetual advertisement seven months out of the year," Vikki enlightened her with a smile. "I never fantasized about owning a mink either. It's quite a change from my corduroy car coat!"

"Don't throw the corduroy away." Jerry Corry's deep voice sliced into the conversation long before his tall, rangy figure became visible among the equipment shadows that ghosted the studio. "We may all need to share its warmth. We've got trouble with a capital T."

Her blue eyes blinked in confusion over the PR man's change in attitude since lunch. "The . . . the rating book was wrong? We're not number one?" Vikki inquired in a halting voice.

"No. That's the problem. We are number one and that leaves us wide open to the

38

likes of this." Jerry threw a half dozen issues of *Newsmaker* magazine onto the oak coffee table. "The hatchet job on one of our very distinguished competitors starts on page twenty."

He shoved his hands into the pockets of his cashmere topcoat and paced in nervous contemplation. "The worst of it is, I invited that reporter, Kip Hallen, to spend next week here." His fingers balled into tight fists. "I can visualize it now. He'll come in and play biology lab — dissecting the show, the writers, and the players as if they were formaldehyde-preserved frogs."

Corinne Bradlee, one of the head writers, threw the magazine across the room in disgust. "I was at that network and wrote for that show. Our story lines were not 'tacky or tawdry.' We worked hard to introduce contemporary topics and make people more aware through entertainment. We won two Emmy Awards for our writing and were the first to portray child and wife abuse, using professionals in the psychiatric and medical field for on-camera advice."

Noel Templar's distinctly British-accented voice added, "This . . . this *interview*" — he sneered the word — "with their leading lady has only one point of view — the reporter's. I worked with Myra Thornway in theater. She's a lovely, talented actress. A true professional." The dynamic stage actor currently portrayed Alex Corwin, the patriarch on *Always Tomorrow*. He looked at his associates. "This is utter rubbish. Hallen's turned Myra into a farce, a joke."

"She's also in the hospital." Jerry sighed and shook his head. "They're calling it an accident. One too many Valiums."

"Can't . . . can't you cancel the *Newsmaker* interview?" Vikki demanded. "Close our set to outsiders?"

"Cancel? Close?" the PR man's voice mocked. "Hallen would have a field day with that!"

"We'd look the worse for it, Vikki." Noel gave his young costar a conciliatory pat on the arm. "A reporter of this low a caliber would still write the article. It would be even more damaging, filled with provocative questions that inspired false answers."

Knowing glances and whispered horror stories were traded among the seasoned veterans. To Vikki their reaction seemed like the proverbial molehill into a mountain. Surely Jerry would be able to insure that Kip Hallen printed a truthful article in *Newsmaker*.

Heather Stuart's shrill voice splintered over everyone else's. "When . . . when that reporter comes here, he's going to dig, and dig deep." Her elegantly manicured nails had carved a series of raw, nearly bleeding scratches into her slender forearm. "He's looking for dirt. He wants it. He'll find it." Mammoth gray eyes silently pleaded. "Corinne, write me out. Kill Beth off. I want —"

"Heather, you're talking crazy!" Vikki interrupted the woman's hysterical ramblings. "There's no reason to get so upset. What on earth could this reporter find?" She looked from one ashen face to another in amazement.

Noel stood up, the brown eyes that dominated his hawklike features softening as they surveyed his protégée's consternation. "Vikki, my dear, I think you're the only one here without a secret." A low but harsh laugh escaped him.

"I — I don't understand." She sat in an erect schoolgirl position. "What are you all so afraid of?"

"You're nice. You're clean," Heather interjected angrily. "You've got no dirty secrets, no lies. I envy you." She seemed near the breaking point, her words tumbling out for everyone else to sort. "I've got a record. Police. My real name, my past . . ." Her hands supporting her head, long straight blond hair shielded Heather's lovely face from view. Tears collapsed her final words. "I was a runaway. Lived on the streets. Shoplifted. Stole. I was only thirteen. That was a lifetime ago. Another me. I — I —"

Corinne Bradlee held the sobbing actress in her arms. "The reason I won an Emmy for those child-abuse scripts was . . . was . . ." The dark-haired writer licked suddenly dry lips and took a deep courageous breath. "I was an abused child. The courts played Ping-Pong with my life. Sending me back and taking me away. I'm still in analysis. My children, they . . . they adore their grandparents. Revealing that part of my past would just hurt too many people I love."

"I — I can imagine what that reporter would do if he found out the actor who played Reverend Patrick Malone was having a very long-running affair with a prominent senator's wife and that her last child was his." David Cushing raked shaking fingers through his dark hair.

Noel sighed. "Let's just say there is quite a bit of tarnish on my Emmy Award." He directed his piercing gaze at Vikki. "I have grown children and grandchildren and, frankly, I'm too old to do battle with these lurid tabloids. I'd rather make my appearance on a stage than in court."

Noel's regal silver-streaked head turned toward a quiet Vikki. "I'm afraid our confessions have shocked our pure-at-heart Vixen." His smile held no malice. "True life reaps a more provocative story line than fiction, does it not?"

Vikki's sapphire gaze concentrated on Jerry Corry, who was pretending great interest in the pattern of his silk tie. Comprehension dawned; she more fully understood why a newcomer had been promoted over the more established stars. Why her fellow castmates had encouraged, no — actually *insisted,* that she as Vixen be the sole advertisement for *Always Tomorrow.*

She stood up and moved center stage. Again, as at lunch, all eyes were staring, but this time they watched Victoria Kirkland not Vixen Mallory. "You haven't shocked me." Her voice was calm and firm. "Actually you've given me a wonderful gift — your trust. We've been a family on this set. A sharing, caring, comforting, loving family. And families stick together especially in times of" — Vikki smiled at Jerry — "trouble, even with a capital T."

Arms extended, hands held palm up, Vikki's piercing blue eyes invaded communal souls. "United we stand." Twelve hands piled together in mutual alliance. "There's no way that Kip Hallen will divide us and make us fall, no matter how far he pushes."

Amid a the tearful hugging and kissing, Jerry Corry's thoughtful voice prevailed. "The worst of it is, we still have Hallen to deal with come Monday. That leaves tomorrow and the weekend to decide what to do and how to do it."

Perched on the oak coffee table, Vikki picked up another issue of *Newsmaker*. "That reporter has no idea what it takes to produce a show five days a week. He twists and ridicules everything. I'd like to see how he fares under our eighteen-hour workdays and then having to learn the next day's lines in our leisure time."

Jerry snapped his fingers. "That's it!" He smiled at their confused faces. "Corinne, why don't we write Mr. Hallen into our show this week? A few lines, and scenes every day. I'll make sure the director has him go over and over his lines until we could all scream. But I guarantee this reporter will learn a lesson."

"Won't that just give him greater access

to all of us?" Heather interjected. "Having him around . . ." She shuddered, burrowing her back into the uncomfortable corner that was the sofa.

"Not if we have a" — his dark gaze focused on Vikki — "red herring."

"I — I beg your pardon?"

"Do you remember those two ladies at lunch today?" She nodded. "They were convinced you were Vixen Mallory. Hallen wants dirt, we'll manufacture a scandal for him. We'll give him Vixen."

"Wait a minute!" Vikki jumped to her feet, her clenched fingers filled with Jerry's tan cashmere coat. "Weren't you the one telling me to protect Vixen. Guard her with my very life."

"You're not seeing Jerry's brilliance." Noel wagged an encouraging finger at the PR man. "Vikki, what's your deepest, darkest, most perverse secret?"

Even white teeth pawed for a moment against full lips. "I — I once stole a yo-yo from a toy shop when I was six. My mother made me give it back to the manager."

"That's it?" Jerry looked pleased. "Marvelous. Hallen will eat it up. I can see the headline now." His hands splayed like a window. "TV's Video Vixen's path to stardom paved in thievery."

"Jerry!"

"Not content to steal trinkets," the PR man continued, "Vixen-Vikki soon began to steal hearts. Masculine hearts. She uses men as a convenience."

"Like a black widow spider" — Corinne Bradlee fumbled in the pocket of her navy blazer for a notepad and pencil — "enjoying then destroying and devouring."

"I like that." Jerry grinned. "You see, Vikki" — he gave her an outrageous wink — "all it's going to take is a little help from your family."

Arms folded across her chest, Vikki looked from one smiling face to another. "In other words, Victoria Kirkland will cease to exist. Vixen Mallory reigns supreme."

"We're two months early for the Ides of March," Noel added smoothly, "but Kip Hallen will get the same greeting as Julius Caesar."

"What . . . what happens to me when the *Newsmaker* story breaks?" Vikki demanded of Jerry.

"That's when we'll launch an all-out campaign for Vikki. I'll book that Donahue show, Merv, Johnny, other magazine and newspaper interviews. We'll show everyone just how great this cast's acting ability is and that 'love in the afternoon' is an industry impossible to degrade." Jerry's hands cupped her face. "Vikki, you'll come out of this a star."

"An actress," Noel corrected, kissing the top of her cold hand.

"As long as everyone backs me up!" Vikki garnered a chorus of promises. "What's this reporter look like? I should at least know the man I'm supposed to enjoy, destroy, and devour," she added on a wry note.

Jerry coughed. "Well . . ." He cleared his throat again. Dark eyes shifted to study the toes of his shoes. "Hallen's about five foot, bushy red hair, thin lips, one eyebrow, no neck, and has chronic bad breath."

Vikki groaned. "I know a girl has to kiss a lot of toads before she finds her handsome prince, but that's ridiculous!" She hid her face in her hands.

"Well, you're home early tonight, Mr. Falkner." Mrs. Horton took possession of two briefcases while her employer removed his snow-damp topcoat. "A little homework?" She placed the cases to one side of the antique hallstand.

"Lots." His large palms wiped the moisture from his gray hair. "Mrs. Horton" —

47

Dan favored his auburn-haired, wiry housekeeper with a smile — "what do you think of the daytime soap operas?" he inquired, taking a rolled magazine from his pocket and following her into the living room.

She looked over her shoulder at him and sniffed. "Don't you think this apartment keeps me too busy to sit in front of the TV all day?" Her arms gestured every which way. "You've got two bedrooms, two baths, a kitchen, a dining room, and this huge-living room. I do all your cooking, cleaning, and laundry and at four I head home to do my own." Mrs. Horton sniffed again, pulling at the flowered bib-style apron that covered fashionable gray wool slacks and a white sweater. "Scotch on the rocks?"

"Please." Dan collapsed his tall frame into an oversized black leather recliner. He gratefully nodded his thanks for the drink. "I meant no disrespect." His calm voice sought to soothe the matron's fractured ego. "I'm trying to get background material for a story I'm doing on *Always Tomorrow* and —"

"*Always Tomorrow*! Why didn't you say so?" Mrs. Horton walked back to the carved walnut cellarette and poured herself a shot of whiskey. "Now that's a show!" She took a healthy swallow of her drink before sniffing again. "I take my lunch hour then."

"Apparently everybody does," Dan concurred, his brown eyes lowered to the men's magazine cradled in his lap. "Vixen Mallory?"

Mrs. Horton groaned and rolled her eyes. "She is aptly named!" She added a second dollup of whiskey before settling her thin frame on the edge of the earth-toned tweed sofa. "I first started watching to see Noel Templar." She patted her heart.

"I saw him on Broadway in the revival of *Macbeth*. Even in tights he's so dynamic, so virile, so much a man." Mrs. Horton cleared her throat and ruffled the wispy bangs that covered her low forehead. "He plays Alex Corwin on the show. Alex is wheelchair-bound, but lately" — she wagged a warning finger at her interested employer — "all that therapy seems to be doing some good." Her voice dropped to a furtive whisper. "I saw him taking some practice steps yesterday."

Dan coughed and cleared his throat. "Why should that surprise you? Templar isn't handicapped."

"Well . . ." she sniffed, fingers pleating the skirt of her apron. "Well of course I know that." Mrs. Horton let the whiskey bathe her parched throat. "Noel Templar is a great actor," came her sudden rejoinder. "He makes me believe he's paralyzed just the way I *know* Vixen Mallory is a man-eater."

"Tell me about Vixen."

The housekeeper crossed her legs. "She was literally dumped in Sodom's Crossing by some no-account womanizer. I felt sorry for her. Poor woman. Used and abused then tossed away." Mrs. Horton gave a derisive snort. "But, oh, my, how she has changed! Vixen managed to get a job as an interior decorator, which of course gave her access into everyone's home. Alex Corwin just fell in love with her, and what man wouldn't?"

Dan sat up straight and disciplined himself to follow the woman's rapid account. "Of course Vixen is just using him as a stepping stone," Mrs. Horton continued, gesturing with her now empty shot glass. "She's really after his son. A blond beach-boy hunk who refused to go back to college after spending the summer with his father and his new stepmother. And then there's Reverend Malone. I know he's got

50

eyes for her, and the doctor, and Corwin's business partner. He's one to watch. He was on the phone today with some mystery man — I think a hit man." Her brown eyes were wide with warning.

Mrs. Horton took a deep breath and continued. "Now Vixen's trying to drive her sister-in-law insane. That woman is so clever, it's frightening. What she gets away with! Of course there's no censors on cable and they all run around practically naked. Even the men. Of course the son, Robert, he looks marvelous in those teeny tiny bikini underpants." She sighed again, lifted her glass, and frowned when she found it was empty.

"You've certainly painted an interesting picture of life on *Always Tomorrow*," Dan was finally able to interject. He looked at his watch. "I don't want to keep you, Mrs. Horton. The weather wasn't doing too well."

Mrs. Horton placed her empty glass on the end table and walked only a bit unsteadily toward the hall closet for her coat and boots. "I left a small pot of beef stew warming on the stove; there's a salad in the fridge and coconut cake."

"Thanks." Dan leaned forward in his chair. "Mrs. Horton, would you mind recording that soap for me tomorrow? That's the only episode I'll get to see before I go to the studio on Monday."

"Certainly." She paused in the open doorway. "Could you get Alex Corwin's autograph for me?"

"I'll try." Dan smiled slightly, noting his housekeeper asked for the character's autograph rather than the actor's. Was it so easy for people to confuse one with the other? That might be an interesting slant to the article.

The gold and black holiday cover on *Playboy* magazine beckoned. Like every other normal, healthy male, Dan started reading the magazine in the middle. Reading? Staring. The girl in the triple foldout was a stunner. A natural blonde, firm full breasts, impossibly small waist, long slender legs. Between the centerfold and the data sheet little was left to the imagination.

Karen Kathleen Gordon, bust thirty-six, waist twenty-one, hips thirty-four. The five-foot-three, one-hundred-pound, twenty-year-old hailed from Cosgrove, Alaska, but now lived in L.A. Her turn-ons: satin sheets and warm body oil; turnoffs: being ignored and soap operas.

The last made Dan smile. Soap operas.

He flicked back to the index, then thumbed to page 102. A fully clothed Vixen Mallory teased her way across five colorful pages while she dutifully aided a male model out of his holiday tuxedo.

Dan carefully read the accompanying photo caption. "Eighteen million fans have created a new number-one bubble on daytime soaps — *Always Tomorrow*. Cable TV's popularity has taken on more subscribers in the last eighteen months courtesy of Vikki Kirkland, whose portrayal of video's most vital, volatile, vivid vixen has garnered more male viewers than all other shows combined. In an unusual vertical position, Vixen Mallory, a truly scarlet woman, shows us what her well-dressed and undressed man would wear."

General Custer, Dan decided, would have gladly surrendered if Vixen had led the charge at Little Big Horn. The first photos showed her tall figure sheathed in a heart-stopping red chamois dress. The skirt was little more than knee-length fringe that dropped from the hip. The unbuttoned neckline was spangled with feathers that invitingly directed the eye toward subtly revealed full breasts.

He flipped the page and found the male model had lost his jacket, tie, and shirt while Vixen had acquired a sequined charmeuse T-shirt worn over matching silken pants. The next photo had her in a long, lean, sensuous wrap dress of fiery cashmere, dark hair piled in a froth of curls that framed a remarkably innocent face despite the fact she was holding a pair of man's pants.

The lady looked a vamp draped in scarlet satin, slashed to the waist, a provocative length of leg bending through a thigh-high front slit, fingers locked around the waistband of a pair of occupied navy briefs.

According to the limited printed information, Vixen-Vikki was ten years older, four inches taller, thirty pounds heavier, and measured two inches larger in all dimensions than the magazine's current centerfold. Yet this mature, clothed brunette disturbed and excited his hormones in more ways than the naked nymphet ever could.

Dan's mind became an erotic messenger; his gaze caressed the lush curves displayed by a sassy black and red glitter teddy reminiscent of the Parisian saloon girls. Vixen's icy blue eyes and wicked smile were effective stimuli to Dan's body so that just sitting became quite painful.

An aura of sexual elegance seemed to surround Vixen. While she was decidedly naughty — pouring champagne into a man's Gucci loafer — she looked nice! Not Vixen — Dan gave his silver head a sharp shake — Victoria Kirkland. Even he was having trouble keeping the actress and the character separated.

Again his eyes stalked the sassy, saucy, scarlet lady that livened the glossy pages. Dan found it was frightfully easy to become Vixenized!

CHAPTER THREE

"It's worse than I thought." Opening the door, Jerry Corry pushed Vikki back inside her small dressing room.

"What could be worse than a bushy, red-haired dwarf with one eyebrow, no neck, thin lips, and perpetual halitosis." Her body shivered beneath the floor-length jet black kimono. "I had nightmares all weekend just trying to psych myself into being civil to the man, let alone vamp him!"

"Now you can have daymares. Kip Hallen didn't show up this morning. *Newsmaker* sent an investigative reporter." He handed her a printed business card.

"Daniel W. Falkner." She tapped the card against her chin. "Why does that name ring a faint bell?"

"He's the global news correspondent who won all those awards for reporting in the world's hazard zones.

Laughing blue eyes snagged brown in the bulb-lit makeup mirror. "They sent the right man," she agreed with a low chuckle.

"We'll make Daniel W. Falkner feel right at home in our own little hazard zone."

Jerry wiped perspiration-damp palms against his tan corduroy jacket. "I don't like it." The heels of his shoes rang against the black asphalt tile. "Hallen I knew we could gaslight, but Falkner —"

Vikki tried to rub some warmth into her numb arms. "Maybe he came because of that awful article in Sunday's *Times* that linked soap operas to everything from increased suicide rates to teaching teen-agers an inaccurate view of adult sexuality."

"Yeah, you might be right. Maybe they just want to hear our side of the story." Jerry made a valiant effort to convince them both. "That article was full of suppositions. Did you see the chart on intimate TV sex acts per hour?" he inquired, letting his nervous frame perch on the edge of her dressing table.

"I noticed we had three point one six," her carefully mascared lashes lowered demurely. "I think the point one six was the encounter between Vixen and the newsboy."

He gave Vikki's nose a warning tap. "Listen, don't get too cocky. Falkner is nobody's fool. When I left him in the green room he was busy filling his notebook with questions."

She eyed the small travel clock that stood boldly apart from the multitude of cosmetics, makeup brushes, and hair appliances that dotted the white marble-topped table. "I noticed he arrived half an hour early."

"That's why I told everyone to be here an hour and a half early," Jerry amended. "It's a little game of check and mate. I had a hunch they'd try to catch us off-guard." A broad grin creased his angular face. "I'm pleased the way everyone has pulled together. The cast, crew, writers — all for one and one for all." He took a deep, fortifying breath. "You know we just might pull this off after all."

"We spent all weekend rehearsing this caper." Vikki found it hard to keep the anger out of her voice. Daniel W. Falkner and *Newsmaker* magazine had complicated everyone's already full schedule. Personal time was at a premium. As it was, she had little in the way of an outside life; little time to be Victoria Kirkland. With every passing second she was growing more bitter at the reporter's arrival. He was just another intrusion, an unwanted and unwelcomed inconvenience.

"I better get back to the green room." Jerry ambled over to the door. "I want to lay the groundwork for his focusing the article on you. Give me another ten minutes before you come out."

Vikki picked up the business card. "I wonder what the *W* stands for?"

"Webster. Daniel Webster Falkner," the PR man supplied.

"Lovely." Her pink tongue circled fiery lips. "He won't be as successful as his namesake against our cadre of devils."

The image in the mirror proved quite hypnotic. Her reflection showed dramatically lined eyes, perfectly shadowed and highlighted cheeks, scarlet lips, and chestnut hair formed in a tousled romantic topknot. Her real self ceased to exist; she was now an illusion.

Playing Vixen Mallory always made Vikki smile. That predatory female was her exact opposite. Vikki had always been more victim than catalyst, reacting to circumstances rather than a woman like Vixen, who made things happen.

Being an evil, scheming villainess proved easier than she had thought. Perhaps because her family and friends provided such a happy base. While Vikki had never studied acting, she found intense enjoyment in her new career. Her character had depth and range, every day was a challenge, and, physically and mentally, she thrived on that fact.

Her gaze focused on the script cover sheet. On a normal workday, she like everyone else would still be in a sweat shirt, jeans, and sneakers drinking their wake-up quota of coffee as their acts were blocked out or "faxed" for the day's taping. A one-hour script ran eighty pages, each act between one and fifteen pages, with one to two dozen acts shot each day. *Always Tomorrow* had two taping times — from ten until two and from four until eight.

There was loose order on the set but order nonethelesss. Dress rehearsals were done just before the final taping; stage hands spent taping time setting up the second sound stage. There were over sixty-five people behind the scenes all pulling together to make *Always Tomorrow* come alive in the living rooms of sixteen million loyal viewers.

Sixteen million fans. The responsibility to them was enormous. Vikki took a deep breath and stood up. Vixen Mallory meant everything to them and to her. "The life you save may be your own," came her spoken promise.

She remembered Jerry saying controversy breeds interest, interest begets ratings, ratings keep you working, the producers happy, and the sponsors ecstatic. "Let Daniel Webster Falkner see *only* Vixen Mallory." Vikki prayed and headed for the studio.

"Here she comes." Jerry waved his hand, directing his companion's attention across the bustling studio.

Dan's brown eyes followed her every step. She moved with provocative buoyancy oblivious to the thick ropes of cabling that snaked along the floor. The sultry black kimono titillated her lush figure, hinting at the wealthy treasures beneath. The magazine photos hadn't done her justice, he decided, trying to ignore his body's heightened sensitivity. In the flesh the lady exuded a special radiance.

Of course there was a fifty-fifty chance Victoria Kirkland couldn't walk and talk at the same time, Dan countered silently. The world was full of beautiful women but beauty alone had never been a lure to him. Intelligence, sensitivity, wit — those attributes he found more attractive than surface perfection. Who knows, maybe she needed a prewritten script to get through a nonworking day.

Vikki's progress slowed slightly; initial shock registered through her brain. Why on earth had she expected Falkner to resemble Hallen? Talk about night and day!

Daniel Webster Falkner proved a savory enemy, at least in the looks department. An impeccably tailored gray pinstripe suit set off his tall, broad-shouldered physique; thick silver hair sculpted a masculine head, proving an attractive contrast to somewhat boyish, rough-hewn features.

A small sigh escaped Vikki. She had spent the weekend gearing up to face a toad and now found she had a handsome prince. The toad would have been more palatable. She could have dissociated herself from someone physically indigestible.

Then again, Vikki rationalized, perhaps that was Mr. Falkner's only claim to fame. That was often the case with a handsome man; they lacked character and substance, letting their looks propel an otherwise empty cockpit.

Jerry made the necessary introductions, deliberately mixing up her name. "With Vikki it's nearly impossible to tell when she isn't being Vixen." His elbow suggestively nudged Dan's.

Rouged lips formed a kissable moue. "Now, Jerry, you know I'm a student of Will Rogers." Dark lashes enticingly slanted blue eyes toward Dan. "I never met a man I didn't like." Feminine fingers conquered masculine in greeting. "Cold hands, warm heart?" Vikki's throaty voice asked the provocative question.

"Depends on who's doing the defrosting." Dan found he was a willing victim of piercing blue eyes that made him positive he was the only man in the room.

Her melodic laugh was backed by a sudden impetus to better know this man. Black python-skin pumps brought Vikki close against his virile frame. Her feminine curves whispered a flirty message. "I'd love to have a chance to disprove that old wives' tale."

"What . . . what old wives' tale?" He cleared his throat, trying to ignore the lust that stirred involuntarily within his body. He was nervous and stammering, like a schoolboy about to lose his virginity.

Scarlet fingernails drew sensual squiggles against the fleshy mound of his thumb on Dan's still captured hand before walking up his arm, over his shoulder, and up to his nape. "The one that goes where there's snow on the roof" — Vikki's fingers filtered through the damp silver hair that coiled against the collar of his ivory shirt — "there's no fire . . ." Her palm flattened against his chest, moving down his rugged torso until she anchored her thumb on his belt. ". . . in the hearth." Her nail suggestively clicked against the brass buckle.

Dan was at a loss for coherent words. This was the first time he had ever been approached as a sex object. He found the position as enjoyable as the woman who bestowed the honor. His eyes devoured her vigorous, wholesome beauty; his nose was taunted by her mysterious Oriental perfume; his ears still rang with a voice smooth as the rustle of satin sheets.

"Daniel" — her fingers flipped up the end of his blue polka-dot tie — "if you keep looking at me like that, we'll be lighting a bonfire in no time." She had him hooked, never underestimating the power of packaging!

He cleared his throat and straightened his tie. "I . . . I was telling Jerry." In mentioning the PR man, Dan quickly returned to reality but found he and the actress were quite alone. "Well, I told Jerry that I was interested in basing my article on how different the actors and actresses are from the characters they portray." He gave her an easy smile. "My housekeeper gets Noel Templar and Alex Corwin confused all the time. I would imagine the public identifies Vixen as a man-eating nymphomaniac and incorrectly assumes so is Vikki Kirkland."

"I am quite the connoisseur of men." She sucked her index finger, pulling the digit ever so slowly from between full, ruby lips. "When I see one I like, I just can't help myself." Vikki's brow arched invitingly. "And I like *you,* Daniel." She crooked her finger and bade him to follow.

Dan tripped over some cabling, his eyes more interested in the embroidered red dragon that breathed fire across the back of her ebony kimono. "Thank you. But . . ." He gave an apologetic laugh.

She led him behind a piece of scenery to an obscure, secluded corner. "There. We won't be disturbed back here." She settled on a cushioned folding chair and gestured him for him to occupy the adjoining one. "You're not married, are you?" A small worry-line creased her smooth forehead. That would really put a kink in their well-laid plot.

"Divorced."

"Presently involved?"

"No." He became hypnotized by the length of bare leg exposed in the opening of her robe. Wondering what, if anything, was underneath became an all-consuming thought!

Vikki leaned toward him; her hand squeezed his thigh. "Why the *but,* Daniel?" She looked like an injured child. "Don't you like me?"

"I don't *know* you."

"That's a problem we can easily rectify." She relaxed against the chair back and smiled. "How long do you have to research your article?"

"Two weeks, more or less." He reached for the slim reporter's notebook inside his jacket pocket. "I do have quite a few of your castmates to interview" — Dan began leafing through inked pages — "writers, directors, producers, and the six major stars of *Always Tomorrow.* Our readers are just waiting to learn all your secrets."

The hell they will! Vikki's interested expression held no hint of the devious plans whirling in her brain. "Daniel, you'd become thoroughly exhausted running around trying to talk to everyone" — her knuckles caressed his powerful jaw line — "and how much fun could we have if you were tired all the time?" Vikki pretended to ponder the problem for a moment. "I'm sure I could answer all of your questions.

Wouldn't you and your readers enjoy a more *intimate* profile instead of such a scattered approach?"

Lady, I would love to go one-on-one with you. I'm still not convinced you're the torrid trapper you're pretending to be. Dan gave her his most charming smile. "It's interesting that you should suggest that. Jerry also mentioned focusing the article through Vixen's" — he shook his silver head — "I'm sorry, I mean through your eyes, Vikki. I'm sure your millions of loyal fans would love to get to know the real you."

The poor duped devil! For a moment Vikki relished the success of Vixen's personality; she thrilled at the ease with which she was able to manipulate this man. But the inherent niceness that was Vikki began to seep through. Daniel Webster Falkner hadn't really been given a chance.

Blue eyes softened as they surveyed his preoccupied features. Vikki found his easy smile and quick wit enormously attractive. The crow's feet that etched his brown eyes enhanced his appeal, as did the truant silver wave that fell against his forehead. The man appeared to be a decent, likable human being.

Dan knew he was being watched, but he continued to check his notes, seemingly

67

oblivious to his feminine inspector. So far Vikki had been in control, making all the first moves. He was enjoying himself and her. But now it was time to turn on the heat, see how the vixen faired when the water boiled.

"As the show's main perpetrator of often deviant sexual behavior, don't you feel some social responsibility for this gratuitous portrayal?" His expression and voice was totally deadpan.

Vikki blinked and swallowed. *So much for Mr. Nice Guy!* She buffed her fingernails against one wide black silk sleeve. "To my knowledge not one complaint about my more sensual scenes has been received. Viewers must feel they are perfectly acceptable." Her blue gaze was quite intense. "Are you making a complaint, Daniel?"

He winced and rubbed his face. "I must admit I've only been privy to one show, and that was last Friday's." His mouth twisted in a crooked grin. "You looked quite . . . um . . . enticing in that black lace" — his hand waved in confusion — "whatever."

"Why, thank you, Daniel. Did you dream about me?" Vikki subtly shifted her position, making the robe's low V-neckline gape slightly.

"Wasn't that what I was supposed to do?" he parried on an even note. "Fantasize over the illusion you as an actress created?" Dan tried to remain focused on her face, but his eyes turned traitor. They discovered more lush enticement in the visible hollow and swells that delineated firm, full breasts.

An unusual recklessness invaded Vikki; her blood became carbonated, shooting through her veins like intoxicating champagne. "I'm no illusion, Daniel." Her fingers gripped his wrist, lifting and placing his hand inside her robe. "Feel my heart." Blue eyes locked into brown. "Am I not real?"

Dan's calloused palm flowed against the velvet that was her breast. Between his fingers her erect nipple palpitated in echo to his own pulsating need. His head bent toward hers. He found he was anxious to taste the reality of berry stained lips.

Vikki could have easily snapped the moment and destroyed the magic. But she didn't. The second his mouth claimed hers, she knew instant gratification. For some unknown reason Daniel Falkner energized her emotions, sparked her spirit, and aroused her body. Her body — not Vixen's. Vikki became the relentless aggressor, her alter ego forgotten.

Her teeth nibbled firm masculine lips apart; her tongue made a quick, tantalizing foray into his mouth. Anxious fingers slipped open the buttons on his jacket, palms pressed against warm fabric-covered flesh in healthy appreciation of his sinewy male form.

His tongue toured the moist crevices of her mouth, savoring her honeyed juices as if they were rare wine. Her sleek fragrant skin provided the seductive energy that fueled his desire. His hand cupped her left breast, enjoying its burgeoning arousal while calloused fingers teased the hardened peak. Where their bodies touched they seemed electrified.

Then suddenly Dan remembered exactly where he was and broke their intimate connection. He shook his head to clear it, wondering how he could have forgotten the sixty people shouting at one another while they busily moved cameras, adjusted lights, and relocated scenery. When he looked into Vikki's glowing face and sapphire eyes, he *knew* how.

"I — I'm beginning to doubt my own sanity," came his hoarse admission. "I'm supposed to be conducting a very impartial interview."

"I'm not going to let you be impartial, Daniel. I want you totally involved." She watched with amusement as he straightened his tie, picked up his fallen notebook, and sat farther back in his chair. Vikki didn't bother to rearrange the front of her kimono, the tie belt held the black silk together at a most dangerous angle.

He decided to get back to business. "Where are you from?"

"Connecticut."

"What part?"

Vikki looked down at herself then at him. "All of me."

The point on his felt-tipped pen was mashed against the paper. Dan threw back his head and laughed. "Lady, you are good. Very, very good."

Putting her hand on his shoulder, Vikki moved her face against his, her mouth a scant inch from his ear. "When I'm bad, I'm even better." Her teeth gave a playful nip to his earlobe.

"You seem to be working awfully hard to convince me you *are* Vixen Mallory." He continued to stare straight ahead, trying to concentrate on the back of a nearby wall flat.

"Don't you believe in typecasting?" Her warm breath tickled his inner ear. "Now,

Daniel, ask yourself this question — would the producer on this program hire an insipid little nothing to play Vixen? You couldn't fool the public. They're more fascinated by a wicked woman than the girl next door.

"Good girls finish last, Daniel, and I've always been at the head of the class. The innocent, wide-eyed, breathless maiden is no longer the draw. The mature woman has the erotic edge. We're more adventurous; we savor and enjoy our sensuality. And what's even more important" — her lips placed a tender kiss on the corner of his jaw — "we know how to please a man."

"The name Victoria was a complete misnomer in your case," came Dan's slightly hoarse rejoinder. His necktie had grown tight and he was having difficulty breathing. This lusty lady was quite a handful.

"Vikki! Ah, here you two are." Jerry Corry smiled a greeting. "Vikki, the director is ready to shoot that tag for today's show." He tapped his watch. "We've got to give the videotape editor time to patch it in," he added before heading back to the control booth.

She slid her hand into Dan's. "Come and watch. I'm sure your readers would like to know how the show is put together."

When Dan returned to the main set he found a backyard patio scene had been constructed complete with trees, grass, flowers, and slanting sunshine courtesy of the lighting man. "Hard to believe the temperature out side is twenty degrees."

"This is Sodom's Crossing, Daniel." Vikki's hand slid possessively along his jacketed arm. "We're slightly below the equator. It's always hot here." She gave him a flirty wink.

"Tell me about the tag you're doing." He tried rather unsuccessfully to hide a smile.

"Just ten seconds to top today's show. I'm to be sunbathing on the patio while someone is watching me through binoculars." Untying her robe, Vikki gave an exaggerated gasp. "Silly me, I forgot to put on my swimsuit." Lashes fluttered in rehearsed confusion. "Don't you move, I'll be right back."

Dan took a deep breath. Now he knew what was not under the slinky black kimono. With supreme effort his brown gaze returned to survey the stunningly real summer set.

So much of television was fantasy and illusion, video magic that created truth from lies. There was no Sodom's Crossing somewhere south of the equator, just a studio set in midtown Manhattan.

It's not what you see, it's what you think you see. A wry smile etched his craggy features. Like beauty, wickedness lies in the eye of the beholder. One man's madonna is another man's whore. Vikki Kirkland had yet to *prove* she was either.

Dan found he was quite content to let Vikki take the lead in this game, let her make all the moves. What the hell! To be honest, he was having the time of his life!

CHAPTER FOUR

"You're doing beautifully, Vik; you've got Falkner in the palm of your hand."

Walking past Jerry, Vikki collapsed onto the tufted coral boudoir stool in her dressing room. "I have him preoccupied with my cleavage and the split in my kimono," came her amended answer. She stared at the PR man's image in the makeup mirror. "Besides being the bait in this little scam, I can't decide whether I'm the fish or the fisherman." Vikki swiveled around, her expression thoughtful and serious. "I *think* I've got Daniel Falkner hooked, but he could be playing with me, tiring me out for the landing."

Jerry moved behind her. "Take it easy." He massaged her shoulders as if she were a prizefighter between rounds. "Relax. Don't sabotage your own talents." His fingers strove to work the tension from her neck. "How about letting him run with the line? Ease up a little on being Vixen, lull him into a sense of false security, and then yank the hook deeper."

Her lips bubbled against an exhaled breath. "I was thinking about doing just that. No sense in going too far, too fast, too soon."

"Atta girl!" Jerry gave her shoulders a confident, final squeeze. "I'd better get back and keep our fish occupied. We can't let him trip up any of the crew."

Elbows on the dressing table, chin propped in her palms, Vikki found the reflection in the mirror anything but enamoring. Oh, the surface packaging was still at its provocative best. But inside, where it counted, she felt gaudy and vulgar. What made matters worse, Vixen Mallory had little to do with those feelings.

Topaz-shadowed eyes taunted in silent ridicule as did a sneering inner voice. *Weren't you just a bit too randy and bumptious?*

"Intensely involved and excited," Vikki countered out loud. "I just got caught up in the make-believe and let myself go."

And you were the one who said a handsome face and rugged body meant nothing!

"So I lied. What of it? Dan's not all flash. You know that. He's got a sharp mind, a quick wit, and I like the fact he's a little shy, a bit reticent. He's refreshing. Those lady-killing Don Juans with the Mr. Macho personality always gave us a headache, remember?"

And what about all that physical contact? You? A true Victorian Victoria?

"Don't be such a prude," she returned on a brusque note. "I wanted to touch him. I wanted to taste him. I'm not going to apologize." Vikki's eyes narrowed in defiance. "The mind is the body's most sensitive erogenous zone. For some reason Daniel Webster Falkner revitalized that zone. I have wants and needs; every woman does. So I took the lead in asking for some momentary satisfaction." Her fingers deftly pulled at the chestnut curls that tumbled against her forehead. "Big deal! Maybe I'll ask again."

Good. It's about time. You've been the celibate Victorian Vikki for too long.

"Hypocrite!" Vikki let loose a Bronx cheer, grinned, and felt much better.

Standing, she shrugged off her robe and tied the neck straps on a bathing suit that had been in place but slightly out of position the whole time. The crimson maillot's ruffled, waist-plunging neckline and high French-cut legs silhouetted her nearly perfect hourglass proportions. "Back to pleasure . . . er . . . business," came her wry directive.

"No. I'm sorry." Dan laughed, cleared his throat, and shook his head. "You've got to be crazy!"

"There's nothing crazy about it. Here's a chance to give your readers a better insight into how daytime TV operates," Jerry Corry continued in his most persuasive manner. "You've got your union card; you can be in the enviable position of being our first celebrity extra."

"Celebrity extra? Jerry, now I know you're insane. Union card notwithstanding, there is no way I'll do it."

"Daniel" — Vikki's hand flowed along his shoulder blade to curve in a warm caress against the back of his neck — "what is it you won't do?" Her purring inquiry vibrated into his inner ear.

Jerry was the first to answer. "I suggested that he might like to become a cast member for the next two weeks. An extra didn't show this morning. Dan could easily do the role, learn how we work, and write from firsthand knowledge." He pressed the rolled script into the reporter's hand. "You play all your scenes with Vikki."

Dan tried hard to ignore the shivery-sensations that feminine fingers were creating against his jaw line. "Ex-exactly what would I have to do?"

Vikki pressed close against Dan, her skin enjoying the rough appeal of his wool jacket. "You play a hired killer," she told him. "You watch me, wait for the right moment and then —"

His head turned in disbelief. "You're getting killed off?"

"No, Daniel," she smiled, luminous eyes wide and guileless. "I get to kill the killer."

"Oh."

"Don't look so sad." Her fingernail outlined his firmly molded mouth. "You die in bed, with a smile. That I guarantee."

Insinuating herself between the two men, Vikki focused the whole of her attention on Dan. "Give it a try." Her dark lashes fluttered in silent encouragement. "Do today's opening teaser and see just how *easy* it is."

"The camera will be aimed just over your shoulder; only the back of your head and an arm will be seen," Jerry inserted quickly. "Your face will be obscured by binoculars. Do the lead teaser, then if you decide not to continue, you'll get the daily pay rate and the director will put in another call for an extra."

"Please, Daniel." Vikki's sultry voice cajoled, "All it takes is an able-bodied man." Her fingers jumped from dot-to-dot on his tie. "And I know of no more abler a body than yours."

As his fervent gaze slid from her alluring face to follow the plunging neckline on her swimsuit, Dan heard himself say in a guttural tone, "What the hell! Why not."

Jerry exhaled a nearly cyanotic breath and snapped his fingers for the stage manager. "Okay. Let's get this man ready for the opening leader."

Dan felt like a sugar cube left on a picnic table — swarmed by ants. Someone yanked off his winter-weight jacket, another rolled up his tan shirt sleeve, still another applied Pan-Cake makeup to his right arm, the back of his neck, and the right side of his face. A stagehand relocated him behind a papier-mâché boulder and a bushy, artificial pineapple palm tree. Black binoculars were slapped into his hand.

During a momentary respite he looked for Vikki. Dan discovered the actress standing in a blue plastic basin. The Hudson sprayer, a powerful water-jet, was in the process of saturating the provocative crimson maillot, rendering the thin fabric almost into a second skin.

"Stop and spot." A nameless member of

the crew reappeared, checked the light meter against various parts of his anatomy, repositioned him slightly to the left, and adjusted the boulder to the right. "Just hold the binoculars in this position."

Dan did as he was directed, found he was shifted a quarter inch to the left, his right arm moved down and toward his belt. "That's fine, Mr. Falkner. Wait for your cue, then let your index finger move the focus control until you feel me tap the back of your leg. Okay?" At Dan's nod the man spoke into the mouthpiece on his headset. "All set here, Charlie. Is Vixen ready? Stand by, Mr. Falkner. Now!"

Dan slowly rotated the binocular's focus wheel, expecting to see nothing. However, the field glasses were real, the 50mm wide-angle lenses magnified Vikki seven times his normal eyesight. He found he was praying that ten seconds would turn into ten hours.

Vikki's supine figure rested on a yellow chaise, dark glasses perched on her straight nose to shade against the blinding artificial sun. Dan followed a water droplet as it made its way down the slim column of her throat and slalomed the valley between her breasts before disappearing beneath the ruffled flutter at her navel.

"Cut, and that's a take."

It took Dan a minute to realize the ten-second tag had been completed. When he handed the binoculars to the stagehand he was chagrined to find the water droplet he had been following was from his own perspiration-riddled forehead!

"Daniel, you were marvelous." Vikki favored him with a most engaging smile as her hand slid into his. "Come and we'll see the finished product."

Taking his hand, she led him into the windowed gallery of the post-production booth. "The effects bank in the video switcher will let the viewers look through the binoculars with you," Vikki explained, nodding toward a massive control board. "The audio man adds music, creating a feeling of suspense. Our videotape editors make it impossible to tell where the patches are made. Watch the monitor; here comes today's leader."

A wry grin twisted Dan's mouth, the camera-cum-binoculars insert proved to be more intimate than his own wide-angle exploration, giving the TV viewer a heart-stopping journey over Vikki's erogenous terrain.

"What do you think?"

"I think despite the January cold wave,

Bloomingdale's is going to have a run on ruffled red bathing suits by two o'clock this afternoon." Vikki's throaty laugh and scantily clad body touched a libidinous chord.

While the male half of Dan was being compelled by pure lust, the reporter half was operating on interest and intrigue. The whole man found it imperative to get to know this captivating woman much better. "Why don't we go have a quiet lunch and talk."

"Mmmm. I'd love to, but I have rehearsals all this afternoon." The regret in her voice was genuine. Vikki looked at the studio wall clock. "There's sandwich and drink machines in the lounge," she offered.

"That will have to do." His tone echoed hers. "I have a three o'clock meeting back at the magazine myself."

As Vikki led the way out of the production booth, Dan again treated himself to the long beautiful curve of her spine and firm buttocks. For a man who had always professed to finding a woman's brain more fascinating than her body, he had certainly made a 180-degree turn. Of course, countered his silent rebuttal, this lady seemed well endowed in both areas.

"The lounge is through the studio doors

and down the hall to the left," Vikki directed, guiding him to one side and away from a dollying camera. "Let me change this clammy suit for my next outfit."

Dan grimaced at his makeup-darkened arm. "Where can I get washed up?" He lifted his jacket off an empty director's chair.

"There's a men's room next to the lounge," she called, padding barefoot toward her dressing room.

Ten minutes later Vikki entered the snack room to find Dan trying to engage a noticeably reluctant Noel Templar in conversation. Straightening the wide black leather sash around her waist, she took a deep breath. *Vixen to the rescue!*

"Noel, darling, didn't you hear the director trumpeting for you?" Vikki favored both men with a benign smile. "You know how testy Charlie gets when you're not on the set to fax your scenes."

"Thank you, my dear." Noel took a waxpaper-wrapped egg salad sandwich from the table. "I'm sorry, Mr. Falkner, but" — he gave the reporter a weak parting handshake — "the show must go on." His grateful gaze focused on Vikki. "Perhaps you'll be able to answer Mr. Falkner's questions for me." The actor's long legs quickly took him from the lounge.

Dan gestured with a paper coffee cup. "I only wanted to ask him for an autographed picture for my housekeeper. She's a big fan."

"How sweet. I'll make sure you get one." Vikki walked toward his table.

"Templar seems a bit nervous." His eyes shifted from the empty doorway to focus on a more gratifying vision. The revealing swimsuit had been replaced by an outfit equally stimulating — a scoop-necked red Angora camisole held by narrow silver straps, and a black silk skirt.

"Preoccupied." She slid into the opposite chair. "He has a heavy taping schedule this afternoon."

"No, he was definitely nervous," Dan persisted, a blunt forefinger tapped the table. "Skitterish, actually."

Vikki toyed with the silver globe dangling from her left earlobe. She strove to sound nonchalant. "Noel is very shy and unassuming; you're *mistaking* that for nerves." She favored him with a winning smile. "Your being here is rather difficult on all of us; we're not used to having outsiders on the set."

"I'm afraid you're going to have to put up with me for a while."

Azure eyes slanted beguilingly into brown. "What exactly are you *afraid* of, Daniel?" Slender bare arms pressed against either side of her unbound breasts to provide an enticing uplift.

The smoky voice and pose was Vixen's, but the heart pounding beneath the overflowing bosom was Vikki's. She knew what *she* was afraid of: her unreasonable fascination with this man.

His thumb bit through the cup, sending a spurt of black coffee over the open notebook. *Keep this up, lady, and we'll soon find out if you're all talk and no action. There's a game afoot here and I'm quite content playing the patsy until I find the answer.* "I'm afraid we had better get some lunch," came his easy answer. Dan stood up and extracted a fistful of change from his trouser pocket. "What will you have?"

She smiled and shook her head, the side fall of chestnut curls dancing against an ivory shoulder. "I'll just let my eyes feast on you."

Dan's choice of ham and cheese on rye was a bland accompaniment for such a naughty lady. "Tell me a little about the actors and actresses on the show." He flipped to a clean page in the notebook. "Noel Templar?"

Vikki leaned against the wooden captain's chair, drying clammy palms against the oak arms. "Noel took his training in England with a Shakespearean repertory company. He was lured out of voluntary retirement by Conrad Garner, who owns the show. He is outstanding in his portrayal of Alex Corwin, and during this season his considerable talents will further enhance our production."

"Heather Stuart?"

"She's a delight. A former model, turned actress. Heather is as sweet as her character. She'll be hosting the Valentine's Day Heart Fund Telethon this year."

"David Cushing?"

"He wanted to get out of the Hollywood rat race, so he came to New York and has been lighting up the TV screens. David is very versatile and loves to play little practical jokes."

"Peter Harris?"

"According to the fan magazines, Peter is this year's 'hunk.' He's just as athletic as he looks. He body builds, plays karate and handball, and does the most wonderful watercolors."

Dan tossed his pencil against the paper and applauded. His sparkling brown eyes baited as did his sarcastic tone. "Very nice.

I could have gotten those same boring stock answers from Jerry's PR kit."

"You asked for my opinion."

"And I got a well-rehearsed, well-practiced one at that, didn't I? I was looking for a little more meat."

Vikki watched as Dan scrawled another note, then slammed his book shut. "Meat? I think you're looking for sauce, spice, flash." Each word was spat with frigid force and condemnation. "What's the matter? Isn't *nice* exciting enough for you. Are your readers bored by *nice* people?"

Ice-blue eyes narrowed in challenge. "We are just that. Nice. People who work eighteen or more hours a day, every day, five days a week, fifty-two weeks a year. Soaps are the number-one form of entertainment in this country — not prime time, not the Super Bowl, not the World Series, or news specials. We are what keeps the networks functioning."

Palms flat on the table, she powered to her feet, her expression carved in stone. "Your reputation preceded you, Dan Falkner. I assumed you would be as impartial on this assignment as you were reporting world events. But you came to do a smear campaign on *nice* people. You and that magazine are so involved with sensationalism, so greedy for the almighty dollar that if you can't find dirt or scandal you'll invent it, allude to it.

"If you're here to try to degrade and defame our show, you won't be able to. The writers have worked on soaps for over a quarter of a century. Each story tries to deliver a moral. We're the Charles Dickenses of our times. The shows are carefully researched and professionally written dramas. Through the medium of television we make people aware of the social mores.

"Yes, some themes are exaggerated. But often that's the only way to get the point across. We show problems and solutions. We are *nice* people who use our talent to entertain."

Hands behind his head, Dan lounged back into the chair. "So you're all *nice*. I wonder. . . ." His dark gaze centered on her anger-flushed features; his voice was low, suggestive, and goading. "Even you, Victoria Kirkland? Has today been one of your more memorable performances as Vixen Mallory?"

Fire-tipped fingers curved like elegant talons, reached out, gripped his tie, and turned it into a silk noose. Vikki hauled a surprised Dan Falkner up from his chair, stopping only when his face was nose-to-nose with hers. "Oh, no, Daniel Webster Falkner, I'm for real." Ruby lips spoke heated words against his mouth. "I'm the spice you're looking for. The only thing you have to *wonder* about is how much seasoning you can handle." Vikki released her hold on his tie; her hands pushed against his shoulders and sent him sprawling backward. "Now, if you'll excuse me, I have to tangle with another man."

Raw nerves fueled by pure adrenaline propelled Vikki to the sound stage. "Charlie" — her breathing came in jerky gasps as she spoke to the bald, casually dressed director — "Steve and I faxed this scene on Friday, and I'm really primed, so can we just go ahead and tape it?"

Charlie stared at her for a long moment, nodded, and began issuing final taping orders as Vikki took her marked position on the office-furnished stage set and spoke to her costar.

Shielded to the left of camera three, Dan quietly watched an unobstructed view of the actors. The scene was between Vixen Mallory and her husband's business partner. A spectacular verbal battle ensued between two stunning performers.

Dan became mesmerized by Vikki's

every word, gesture, and movement. The scene was choreographed so slickly that when the climax came and Vikki was the recipient of a slap that sent her head reeling in a powerful whiplash, Dan jumped toward the stage.

A grinning cameraman halted him and jerked a thumb toward the effects man, who produced the sound that made the blow so realistic. Uncurling his balled fist, Dan had to again remind himself this was all illusion.

With a sharp shake of his head he moved toward the exit door. Looking back at the actress, Dan wondered if illusion and reality weren't one in the same. And if Vikki Kirkland was more Vixen than Victoria, why the hell had he tried to come to her rescue!

"Excuse me, I'm looking for Mr. Falkner?"

A petite young blond receptionist swung around sharply. Her brown eyes widened as they focused on the black mink coat and fingers that had been fumbling with the zipper of a jacket froze. "He's . . . he's back there." She pointed to a distant glass-enclosed corner. "Is . . . is that real?" her awed whisper inquired.

Smiling, Vikki nodded. She watched the young woman's lilac-coated fingernails move cautiously toward her coat sleeve. The receptionist's fingers reverently stroked the luxurious fur and a humble "Thank you" blessed Vikki along her way.

The *Newsmaker* office was populated only by paper-strewn metal desks and mute file cabinets. Vikki's black suede boots moved silently across the heel-marked white tile floor toward her quarry.

She had made a tactical error this afternoon allowing anger to slip Vixen's mask and let Vikki appear. It was imperative for her to regain control, to focus Dan Falkner on certain points only, and keep him deliciously off-balance and confused.

Vikki had yet to decide if she had hooked her fish but had become resolved to the fact her fish provided his own powerful lure. The combination of Dan's physical form and mental quickness had whetted her sensual appetite, an appetite, that had shocked her with its voracity, an appetite that was demanding to be fed.

An smile of irony twisted her claret-glossed lips. It seemed Victoria and Vixen had quite a few things in common. Foremost was a healthy appreciation for an attractive, available man and the self-confidence to pursue him, charm him, and ultimately possess him.

My, my, you've certainly come a long way, baby, an inner voice gave a pleasurable laugh. *You used to be so wimpy, so afraid, so embarrassed — even with Gregg! Why not now? What's this man got that makes you feel so earthy, so provocative, so womanly?*

"I only wish I knew. I only wish I understood," Vikki mumbled out loud. Determinedly she smothered the metamorphosis of unaccustomed emotions that reigned supreme over her normally strictly controlled sensibilities.

Her hand moved to the front of her coat, hovering over the three mink buttons. One by one, Vikki released them and, in doing so, she freed Vixen and the bait that would reclaim her feminine mastery over Daniel Webster Falkner.

Inside the glass-caged office was a scene that made Vikki think of King Arthur and the Knights of the Round Table — twentieth-century-newspaper style. Eight chattering men with rolled-up shirt sleeves sat around a circular table littered with coffee cups, papers, and crumbs from half-eaten donuts.

She focused on Dan Falkner. His back faced her, broad shoulders straining in sinewy movement beneath a tan shirt; his large hands shuffled papers and photographs, an authoritative finger jabbed the air. Vikki studied the silver waves that sculpted against his powerful head; her palms tingled against the memory of those virile coils from their brief encounter that afternoon.

One by one the *Newsmaker* knights noticed the mink-clad woman framed in the glass doorway. Seven pairs of eyes lost interest in editorial duties, concentrating instead on a more enjoyable diversion.

Lifting her hand, Vikki's finger's fluttered in a flirty greeting and she returned seven eager smiles with a seductive one of her own. Light-blue irises slanted in voluptuous contemplation toward the silver-haired editor.

She watched Dan swivel his chair around, his scowling countenance undergoing a transformation from astonishment to an easy grin. To Vikki's own amazement his lopsided, masculine smile sparked all those feelings that were so tritely printed between the covers of a romance novel.

Her pounding heart did seem to turn over and her knees buckled slightly despite the backing of boots; blood coursed through normally undaunted veins in a fevered rush that sent her skin aglow. Who knew the formula for the chemistry that primed a feminine heart? Maybe all it took was a smile from the right man.

Dan Falkner, the right man? In one day? Vikki took a deep, steadying breath; she had long believed in fate and destiny and knew there were some things that couldn't be measured in time. But until she had the opportunity to really think about what she felt, what she needed, and what she wanted, Vikki decided to let Vixen handle the situation.

"Well, this is quite a surprise." Dan firmly closed the office door. "To what do I owe the pleasure of your visit?"

Wine-burnished lips formed a contrite moue. "I came to apologize. I behaved quite badly this afternoon, yelling at you the way I did." Vikki moved close against him; the soft pads of her fingertips gently sought to stroke away the weary lines that etched his mouth.

Delicate fingers continued a suggestive course down the strong column of his neck before rubbing lightly at a red fabric-burn made visible by his open collar and loosened tie. "Dan, did I do that?" This time the remorse Vikki displayed was genuine.

Strong fingers conquered hers. "Could be. You certainly didn't sheath your vixen claws today." Dan's enigmatic expression belied the interest registered in his brown eyes. The more he was with her, the easier it was to tell Vikki from Vixen. Vikki called him Dan while Vixen made two seductive syllables out of his first name. One woman was honest; the other affected. The trouble was Dan discovered he thoroughly enjoyed them both.

Mentally upbraiding herself, Vikki tethered her concern and spoke in Vixen's invidious manner. "You're very lucky, Daniel," came her throaty purr. "I usually leave a more permanent souvenir when I'm in a passionate encounter" — mascara-darkened lashed fluttered suggestively — "even when it's an angry one."

Dan cleared his throat and tried to cultivate the bashful, hesitant image he had been projecting all day. It wasn't as difficult as he expected once he caught a glimpse of what Vikki was wearing beneath the opulent mink. Tucked into a velvet skirt was a sheer, black lace-blouse with tiny, scattered flowers that saved fur-warmed, pink skin from indecent exposure.

Capitalizing on her feminine advantage, Vikki slipped her right hand into the skirt pocket and dragged to one side the coat's wide lapels, allowing Dan to view more of her diaphanously wrapped torso. She would use every available wile to control and direct this reporter. Vikki was still uncertain as to who was the better actor during their tête-à-tête. Men seemed natural actors, so persuasively convincing in getting women to physically prove their love and then being totally uncommitted in the cold light of day themselves. She intended to use every advantage.

With her left elbow resting casually on his broad shoulder, Vikki pressed against Dan's side. Her unbound breasts strained beneath their gossamer covering to snuggle on either side of his shirt-sleeved arm. "I came to invite you to my place for dinner." Her fingernail playfully zigzagged along his jaw line. "After all, isn't the way to a man's heart through his" — her right hand came free of the skirt pocket to draw lazy squiggles along his flat-bellied torso — "stomach." Her thumb booked inside the waistband of his trousers.

A nerve jumped in Dan's eyelid. "I would have never suspected you of being such a homebody."

Even white teeth sank a velvet bite into his earlobe. "I'd just love to have your body in my home." Vikki suppressed a satisfied smile when a low, masculine growl was emitted from his throat. "After dinner we could practice tomorrow's script."

Brown eyes blinked away the staring study of a rose-tipped nipple that had managed to escape its lacy protective covering. "Script?" Dan's mouth twisted into a grimace. "I'd forgotten all about that."

Rolled papers were removed from a fur-covered pocket. "You're in quite a few scenes tomorrow, Daniel. You're expected on the set by six." Vikki slid the script into his hand.

"I'm in an editorial meeting right now that won't break up till nine, then I have a production meeting. I've manuscripts to edit, photographs to approve, and now you tell me I have to be at the studio at six A.M.!"

"Does that mean you can't have dinner with me?"

"No dinner, no snacks, no breakfast." His silver head shook off dizzying fatigue. "I'm not even sure I'll have time to breathe."

Vikki exhaled a tragic sigh. "What a shame! And Daniel, I was prepared to offer you all the snacks and breakfast you might desire. Oh, well" — she gave him an encouraging smile — "the least you can do is walk me to the elevator."

A blunt forefinger stabbed the call button. "Do I get a raincheck?" Dan gauged her reaction.

"You don't have to wait until it rains, Daniel. I thought we agreed this interview was going to have a unique intimacy about it." Eyes that promised pleasure left his to again focus on his neck. A small frown puckered Vikki's smooth forehead; her finger touched his skin. "I am very sorry for this." Vikki bestowed a tender, healing kiss.

She felt his hands slide inside her coat and expertly caress her back. Vikki molded herself to Dan's vigorous frame, her hand pushing his head down to meet hers. The pressure of his mouth was warmly, instantly, stimulating, like a double shot of the finest cognac. Her tongue sampled the texture of his lips and probed deeper into the moist recesses, anxious to seek a mate.

An unusual reckless boldness seemed woven into Vikki's feminine fabric. She decided to just *be*. To take sustenance from this man, to let him energize her very soul.

Her fingers bathed amid the abundant

silver coils that feathered his head. Her body branded its womanly imprint into his. Soft feminine curves cloaked his masculine form in a joyous subjugation.

Dan savored this elegantly wanton ambush. His questing hand confiscated one full breast. His thumb and forefinger found the truant nipple that evaded its delicate covering and teased the soft peak into an ardent nub.

With a little groan Vikki stopped feasting on his masculine lips. "Dan" — fingers pulled the collar of his tan shirt up and down — "couldn't you adjourn your meetings until tomorrow or cut them short?"

He stared into wide black pupils rimmed by sapphires. His answer was totally honest. "You don't know how much I wish I could, Vikki." The opening elevator door announced its presence. "I'm afraid I'm going to have to get back to work and say good night."

"It could have been." Vikki threw him a final kiss and stepped into the waiting hoist.

Dan inhaled a deep, steadying breath. At this point it seemed Victoria Kirkland was more a handful than Vixen Mallory. While four years in the navy had prepared him to meet adventure, he seriously doubted if he could keep all hands on deck!

At the fifth floor, Vikki realized just how little Vixen had been in control. Vikki had reigned supreme. She was no longer a chameleon with no identity. She reveled in her newfound power and was strong enough to trust herself in any situation. She was receptive to new experiences. She was *more* than receptive to Daniel Webster Falkner.

CHAPTER FIVE

"Chin down. Slant those eyes, love. A little more smile. No . . . no, too much. Don't give me teeth, Vikki. Better." *Click, Whirl. Click.* "Much better. Lift your arm over your head. Gracefully, love, you're not heaving a gunny sack." *Click. Whirl.* "Relax a bit. Ruffle the hair. Lick the lips. Turn your head slightly. Yes . . . yes . . . damn, you lost it."

Peter Finch crawled along the carpeted riser on denim-covered knees and ended up resting his square chin on top of Vikki's bare thigh. "From the neck down you are Vixen."

Half-hooded gray eyes became a roller coaster, flowing across the lush curves and angles of Vikki's supine form, derailing over two encounters with charmeuse silk ruffled briefs and a bowtied badeau. "Unfortunately your pensive little mug is ruining the total effect, wasting film and time."

Vikki's head collapsed into a propped black satin bedpillow. "I'm sorry, Peter, I guess I have the Monday-morning blues."

"It's Tuesday, love. You have marvelous thighs." A primitive hissing sound was issued between masculine lips. Peter was about to sink his teeth into inviting feminine flesh when one malevolent ice-blue eye silently dared him. "Spoil sport." Instead, his index finger brushed the blond-brown bristles on his thick mustache. "Want a drink?"

"At ten in the morning?"

"Something inspiring to smoke or sniff?" Again the blue eye stared in mute disapproval. "Victoria, love, how well named you were. Sometimes you can be a bloody shrew without saying a damn word." Peter rearranged his wiry frame Indian-style. "Tell Uncle Pete your problem. It can't be the ad campaign. You did beautifully last week. This photo session should be a throwaway for us."

"I just didn't expect to have to do this again, especially not today." Vikki lay her head on her arms, exhaustion evident in each word. "I faxed scenes from seven this morning until twenty minutes ago; from here I go back to the studio and tape until ten tonight, and at midnight, I film the public service announcements for MADD."

"You do have one helluva day," he grimaced. "Did I tell you I agreed to donate my photographic services to do some MADD posters? I'm putting together a montage for use in high schools and colleges." Peter looked up from checking the motor drive on the Nikon camera and blinked. "Now, why didn't you smile like that five minutes ago?"

Vikki wrinkled her nose at him and playfully tugged one of the tight blond curls that framed his rough-hewn features. "You should have told me that five minutes ago. Peter, you are fantastic. Mothers Against Drunk Drivers is a wonderful and, unfortunately, necessary organization. A poster from prize-winning photographer Peter Finch mounted on school walls will grab the kids' attention and make them think before they get behind the wheel after draining a six-pack. Five thousand teenagers died last year in traffic accidents that involved alcohol." Vikki shivered despite the 1000 watts generated from the quartz lights. "Such a damnable waste."

"Tell me about the TV campaign."

"Three cast members from *Always Tomorrow* and myself are involved. Noel Templar's will be directed toward the senior citizen, not only on alcohol but on eye check-ups as well; Peter Harris's spot is aimed at the eighteen- to twenty-four-year-olds; David Cushing's at women, and mine will stress that *macho* means having the guts to say no to one for the road and not drive when you've been drinking."

The celebrated photographer slanted Vikki a lecherous glance. "You're the perfect choice to make any bloke give up pub-crawling to get bevied on a far more interesting cup." Peter flicked a forefinger toward one red-silk-swathed breast. "Which brings us back to your present position. Last week you posed in black on red sheets; today you are the scarlet woman on black sheets for Vixen perfume." He gave an encouraging smile. "Can't you muster up just a hint of passion?"

"I do better as the lady in blue," came her glum retort.

Peter shook his head, stood up, and switched off the quartz lights. "Take a break, Vikki, there's fresh coffee in the corner. I'm going back to my office and make a few calls, then we'll give it another go."

Burrowing her head into the satin plumpness of the bedpillow, Vikki tried to muster a yawn. Her lethargy, however, was mental, not physical, and totally of her own doing — and wholly due to Dan Falkner.

Poor Daniel Webster Falkner, the man had been strapped to a merry-go-round all last week. When he wasn't tied up with rehearsals *Newsmaker* kept him occupied with assorted daily emergencies and while he was at the studio *Always Tomorrow*'s cadre of devils put him through the wringer. Dan could do nothing right, not in blocking simple scenes or the final taping. He and a skeleton crew stayed long after everyone else had gone home.

I just can't understand this, Vikki remembered him muttering after a tenth retake, *they used to call me one-shot Falkner when I was doing standups on cable news.*

A rueful smile twisted her lips as she recalled last Friday. Dan had been stunned to learn his final scene, the big love-death one with Vixen, would be done *sans* Vikki. "What do you mean I'm supposed to make love to a piece of masking tape on a bed sheet? What happened to die-with-a-smile?" Dan had demanded of her and Jerry Corry.

"You die and smile on cue. We do it all the time," Jerry grinningly assured him. "That's why God made video editors.

Vikki has to shoot the Vixen perfume ads this afternoon. Her part of the scene has already been laid on tape and will later be married to yours. Simple, and it allows a person to be in two places at the same time."

"It'll probably take me one hundred takes to get the proper smile," Dan had complained to her while trying to fit in some interview time. "Daniel, you won't find it difficult if you approach the scene correctly." Vikki had led the disgruntled reporter to the empty makeup room. "Let your mind take control and play off a mental image." She handed him a cup of coffee and gestured toward a nearby chair. "The brain is the body's main erogenous zone. Don't fight it. Work with it. I did." An innocent smile curved her lips. "I just pictured you on the bed, totally nude, and I started at the top and worked my way ever so slowly down."

She didn't touch him. Instead, Vikki let her eyes and her voice become a pair of adventurous explorers traveling over his male anatomy. "I feel akin to Delilah when I run my fingers through your hair. Those thick silver waves invoke a tempered virility that I find enormously arousing." Black-lace lashes enticingly shaded blue eyes. "I'm very anxious to find out if *all* your hair is silver, Daniel.

"Then I moved onto your earlobes. They make a tasty treat." Her tongue ran lightly across her crimson upper lip. "I could spend hours planting little kisses along your cheekbones, your jaw, and tuck a few into the tiny cleft in your chin. And your mouth" — a feline purr escaped — "ummm, warm, wet, wonderful. Lips so firm and commanding. Tongue hard and swift."

Vikki had watched Dan's Adam's apple within his throat in consternation but her sensuous, lyrical voice was never interrupted. "I envisioned myself giving you a massage. There's nothing quite so soothing yet so sensual for both partners. I could actually feel the potent energy harbored in your muscles come alive beneath my hands. My fingers rubbed in ever-widening circles over your back, shoulder blades, then moved with long, sweeping strokes up and down from the base of your neck to your buttocks. Your skin growing warm and slippery from heated cinnamon oil.

"I'd roll you over and work on your arms, torso, and shoulders. Kneading and stroking and massaging. Open palms fanning out across your chest to smooth any tightness. My fingernails would forage through the soft mat of hair, teasing the tough masculine nipples and finally I'd discover whether your navel is an innie or an outie.

"My hands would venture lower, gently caressing and investigating your more pronounced male attributes." Vikki had arched an elegant brow. "So you see, Daniel, when I taped my half of the love scene, you were there. I saw you, tasted you, touched you, and possessed you." She smiled, blithely ignoring his gray-tinted complexion and shocked expression. "I never even noticed the masking tape."

Rolling on her back, Vikki stared up at the ceiling and the black Fresnel lights mounted on the grid. Each light was equipped with a set of barn doors — metal plates that restrict illumination to a concentrated area. Vikki's lips twisted in derisive amusement. Wasn't she wearing barn doors? Hadn't she converged all her energies on Dan Falkner?

During the past week Vikki realized her absorption in the man had little to do with the original "gaslight" project. She was herself rather than Vixen Mallory, and Victoria Kirkland was proving to be quite the hedonist.

What a turnaround for a woman who had always been in total control and never overly emotional. For a woman who always mistrusted the instant rush of attraction and excitement when dealing with the opposite sex. For a woman who always considered herself a sexual cripple in the "age of enlightenment."

SEX! Three little letters that were suddenly capitalized into her brain. Vikki took a deep breath. She had never engaged in casual, carefree, or uncomplicated affairs. She had to care and care deeply, care totally. There had been only one man who had inspired her trust, her affection, her love . . . and that relationship had taken four years to build.

Gregg Chastain. Gregg had been in her thoughts these past few days, but Vikki knew the reason for it. She closed her eyes and found time had blurred his image and healed old hurts. Concentrating harder, Vikki was slowly able to rebuild a four-year-old visual souvenir.

Clean cut, Gregg had been teased about his looks but he was secure enough to defy his peers and keep his sandy brown hair neat and trim. "Who would trust a shaggy, mop-haired doctor?" he'd asked, then his blue eyes would bely his serious voice.

"Besides, if my ears were covered, my stethoscope would be useless."

She had been twenty and in her second year at Newhouse Center for Public Communication at Syracuse University when she'd met Gregg. He was in his second year of pre-med. A very positive, very self-assured *older* man. She had been unimpressed.

"Why did you pick me to interview?" Gregg had demanded.

"I didn't pick you; I pulled your name out of a hat. Everyone in the class is doing an interview with a med student."

"Fine. Come up to the gallery. You can ask your questions while I watch a gall bladder operation."

Much to Gregg's chagrin, she sat through the operation, eyes open and completely unaffected. An hour later, when Gregg sliced open a hot dog and poured on ketchup, she fainted, her head just missing a bowl of soup.

Vikki had never been sure how or why their friendship had continued and developed. They had a lot in common, similar backgrounds, large, loving families, and both were working their way through college. For a long time she regarded Gregg as another brother — teasing, confiding in, and arguing with him. They wrote and called each other over summer vacations and, gradually, after two years, they had a totally monogamous relationship. Their friendship had caught fire, physical fire, and a commitment was made in mind, heart, and body.

Gregg was taking his internship and residency at NYU and Vikki was able to secure a job at an educational TV station in New Haven. She lived at home, saving the bulk of her salary for a dream wedding and spending all her free time with Gregg.

Loving Gregg had made her a different person. She had been what Helen Gurley Brown had aptly described: a mouseburger. Well, the mouse suddenly began to roar. Vikki was filled with energy, excitement, and enthusiasm for the present, and promise, hope, and happiness for the future. The future — what a delicate bubble and one so easily burst.

Vikki abandoned her thoughts of the past to view the present. Funny, her smooth forehead puckered in silent contemplation. She hadn't realized just how "present" she had been living for the last three years. In the beginning she had run minute to minute, minute to hour, hour to day before settling into an established day-to-day routine. Her work had been her focal point, actually her life saver. At night she had dreamed of tomorrow's work.

Last week all that changed. She met Daniel Webster Falkner. The man occupied her every thought, morning, noon, and night, and Vikki found she didn't have to wait until night to dream. His every feature had been seared into her brain; her lips could instantly taste the honeyed delights of his mouth; her nose easily recalled the crisp, outdoorsy cologne he wore.

Always content to sit back and let things happen, Vikki was enjoying her equal right to be assertive. In fact, she was behaving as if she were a law unto herself. For the last five days, she had taken every opportunity to physically tease and sexually entice Dan, but in doing so Vikki found she was only torturing herself.

Dan Falkner had become an obsession. Vikki wasn't man-hungry, she had dated since Gregg, albeit nothing intense. She had sown all the wild oats she intended. She knew what she wanted because she knew what she didn't want. Daniel Webster Falkner contained more pluses than minuses. Their energy seemed to complement each other, his internal while hers external.

Vikki liked Dan's vulnerability, his humor, and his integrity. Integrity — he did have that. Despite the merry-go-round she had skillfully kept him on, Dan was a tenacious interviewer. She remembered another one of their "vending machine" lunches when he had tossed a copy of the University of Pennsylvania's Annenburg School of Communication's report on daytime TV at her and said, "Let's talk about this."

She looked up from her tuna sandwich and smiled. "Oh, yes, they're the group who calculated the number of propositions, kisses, explicit pettings, copulations, rapes, and homosexual acts shown or implied during afternoon programming." Her expression was serene and stoic. "Must have been exciting research. I can just visualize them sitting around four TV sets clicking away on calculators."

"*Always Tomorrow* did lead in the number of intimate sex acts per hour. Two other university studies concur with the statement that heavy daytime TV watching distorts viewers' ideas about adult sexuality." Dan squirted mustard on his ham and cheese before continuing.

"Ninety-four percent of all daytime copulations, are between unmarried people;

114

basically you're providing *lust* in the after-noon with openly displayed seduction, sex running rampant, and one-quarter of the scenes consisting of behavior that is dis-couraged by society, i.e., rape, adultery, and prostitution." Dan added sugar to his coffee, the plastic spoon dripping coffee as he dripped accusations. "They charge sex is a cheap way to get ratings and make a profit."

Vikki swallowed a mouthful of tuna. "Does life imitate art or does art imitate life? Rather like which came first the chicken or the egg?" She eyed Dan with interest. "When you were doing your news stories from Lebanon, did you worry that showing all the fighting, all the weapons and artillery, all the dead bodies would incite same in Buffalo, New York?"

"You're reaching. We were showing news."

"And we're showing entertainment. People use soaps as an escape just like James Bond, Miss Marple, or the Muppets. Despite all the bedhopping, lies, deceit, murder, and amoral behavior, soaps do support traditional moral values. Too much reality is deadly and we provide fan-tasies that someone else plays out."

"Some people can't distinguish between

fact and fantasy,'" Dan pointed out.

"Then I'd be more afraid to have them watch the news or read the papers. Look at all those copycat cases every time some bizarre crime occurs." She shook her head. "Maybe we do provide a little more video foreplay than the networks who have censors, but we have our censors too. When you look at the story in context, you see that every character and action goes full circle and all reap their just rewards."

"What about those who don't stick around to see the soap story come full circle?" Dan turned to a marked page in the bound report. "They cite preteens and teens who get caught up in the soaps during summer vacation. This is the group that has the hardest time separating fantasy from reality. They see sex so freely shown that it loses its dignity and place in life."

"If that group took a bit more time for research, they'd have noticed a change in story lines during the summer months," Vikki told him. "Most of the shows direct a portion of the plot to that sensitive age group. *Always Tomorrow* inserted a runaway into the story, showed what could happen, stressed the runaway hotline telephone number, and we had an actual psychiatrist-counselor on the show talking to the parents. Ask Jerry to show you all the complimentary letters we received."

She watched Dan make notations in his book. "One interesting university study revealed that teens who watch soaps are less likely to use drugs. No, Dan, if I were a parent, I'd worry less about my teenager watching a soap opera and more about peer group pressure and loss of communication in the home. You've got to have confidence in the viewing audience. People are not stupid; they have the intelligence to say enough is enough."

He'd looked impressed. "Can I quote you?"

"Absolutely." She knew Dan would quote her accurately.

On the surface he appeared quite respectful of the actors, writers, and technical crew involved in the show. But everyone, especially Jerry Corry, was still on the defensive, still wary. All had eagerly waited for the next issue of *Newsmaker* only to find a notation bar saying the rest of the soap story would be in two weeks — with an entire edition of the magazine focused on daytime TV.

Vikki had found that disconcerting too. She also found herself wondering about the notes and observations Dan was always jotting in his reporter's notebook — a notebook that was shielded and protected as if it held the secrets of the universe.

Mostly, however, Vikki found herself wondering how to make the next four days last forever. What irony! She had once wished that old proverb "Time flies" would come true. Now she wanted to capture time, make every second of the ninety-six hours she had left with Dan count.

An accident had brought her in contact with a man who felt right. A man who restored her rose-colored glasses. A man who had made her look forward to tomorrow. She desperately wanted him to see the other side of Vikki Kirkland. She was very content with who she was and wondered if she was a woman he could become interested in.

Would it hurt anyone to let her feelings lead the way? She had always said too much, dreamed too much, and done too little. Why not take a chance and go for it? Take dead aim on Daniel Webster Falkner. She'd regret it more if she didn't!

"Vikki, love." Peter Finch's voice ended her musings. "I've got a man here who says you won't mind if he watches our shoot."

CHAPTER SIX

There was nothing tame about the woman reclining on midnight satin sheets. Dan Falkner let his dark eyes travel in lusty deliberation over Victoria Kirkland's vital female form. From the wanton tumble of chestnut curls that titillated bare shoulders and scarlet-silk-bound breasts to the sensuous hip-to-waist curve exposed by flirty briefs, the overall effect was ravishing.

"Hold that pose, love." The clipboard Peter Finch was holding crashed unimportantly against the studio floor. The photographer's wiry frame acted as though it had been energized. One hand grabbed a loaded Leica camera from a table; the other snapped to life the quartz lamps and repositioned an umbrella reflector. "Don't move your head, Vikki. That's marvelous. Wet your lips. Marvelous. Bend your right knee slightly. Marvelous."

A seven-letter expletive was hissed from Dan's clenched teeth. If Finch said "marvelous" one more time . . . His right hand formed a fist that was hurled forcefully into his left palm. That damn man literally drooled the word and turned it into something obscene. Did he have to straddle Vikki to get that shot!

Grudgingly Dan conceded that Finch's work showed unsurpassed skill, imagination, and artistry as did the man's highly touted, rather lurid life-style. The photographer's appetite for models was well known in Manhattan.

Again Dan focused on the model and critically observed Vikki's response. She was flirting — but for the camera or for Finch? Was the flamboyantly sensuous lady in red reacting to the photographer or to the unknown voyeurs who would eventually see this advertisment?

Vikki was enjoying herself. Dan had no doubts about that. Her supine form displayed an elegant vitality that emanated from jewel-bright eyes, radiant skin, and an occasional burst of melodic laughter. He found himself caught up in her excitement. His pulse raged and his blood pressure began to rise. Muscles tensed; sweat beaded his upper lip.

His physical reaction was enhanced by memories of previous encounters. He had sampled the erotic pleasure of her full lips and luscious mouth. His hands and fingers had possessed and intimately explored her breasts. The exotic perfume she always wore taunted him even from a distance, provoking instant arousal.

To be honest, Victoria Kirkland haunted him like a passion. The splendor of her occupied his mind. Compared to Vikki all other women seemed to him to be only half alive. With each passing day Dan found himself growing more susceptible to this scarlet woman, this vixen in ebony.

The lady's favorite colors were so apropos to her personality. Victoria Kirkland was wicked and outrageous, fiery and explosive, yet still shrouded in mystery. She was a puzzle — a true enigma. She was a strong, competent woman who enjoyed herself and Dan found that at once satisfying yet provocative.

Suddenly he realized how frustrated he'd become during the past week. Vikki was always just out of reach, tormenting and tantalizing him. Beguiling light-blue eyes promised so much pleasure; her warm, full-bodied laugh and throaty voice seemed to stir the animal in him.

Frustrating. Dan leaned against a navy-carpeted wall, arms folded across his chest. Yes, frustrating was the word. A lopsided smile twisted his lips. Challenging, too, for

Victoria Kirkland was a natural actress. She always said more than she actually did. A sorceress of magic that stirred his blood, a mistress of sweet illusion that made him submit to anything.

The times he had managed to take control, to deftly probe during an interview he was able to get Vikki to reveal her true self, to let the calculated Vixen facade slip. Dan found her exciting in what she really was rather than what she pretended to be. His nocturnal dreams held up to daytime scrutiny. Victoria Kirkland filled his world with delicious uncertainty.

"I wish Falkner had arrived sooner." Peter's blond eyebrows wiggled suggestively.

"Why say that?"

He rearranged the angle of Vikki's shoulders. "You came alive the minute you saw him."

"I don't know what you're talking about."

"Lying does not become you, Victoria." *Click. Whirl. Click.* "I saw the difference and so did this." Peter tapped the camera housing. "The lens doesn't lie even if the lady does." Gray eyes stared into blue. "You've got that special radiance that has a decidedly sensuous appeal. I'm jealous. You've been saying no to my cleverest propositions for the last three weeks. What's this bloke got that I haven't? What's his technique? Give Uncle Pete a hint. It's only fair. My ego has been badly bruised."

Her pink tongue protruded between berry-glossed lips. "Suzy's column in the *Daily News* pictured one Peter Finch with his celebrated arm draped around an adoring blond nymphet who I bet is doing a wonderful job caressing your bruised ego," came Vikki's smiling rejoinder. "As for Dan Falkner" — she looked beyond the photographer's shoulder to focus on the man in question — "he rather inspires propositions."

Peter turned for a cursory inspection. "Really. Now, that's an approach I never thought of trying. Make the ladies do all the work. Interesting." He peered at Vikki through the viewfinder. "And how are you making out?"

She giggled at his choice of words. "I'm rather new at this. Luckily Dan's a slow starter." Vikki slanted a vixenish glance at the photographer. "But I'm betting we'll both go the distance." *As long as I have the courage of my convictions,* she amended silently.

"Hold it." Click. "That's it, love. Beautiful." Peter collapsed in an exhausted heap on the edge of the prop bed. "This is the best in the series. I think I'll invite Falkner every time I need to shoot you."

Vikki sat up. Her fingernail scratched a light warning rasp against his beard-rough jaw. "Don't you dare." Despite her easy smile the words were delivered with force.

He exhaled an exaggerated sigh. "Just trying to lend a hand," Peter returned innocently, his knuckles tracing the curve of her waist. "A frustrated model is not conducive to business and I might just learn something."

"You're more the teacher than the pupil, Mr. Finch."

"Where and what time are you filming the MADD spots tonight? Just to show you my good side, I'll come down and snap some stills for posters."

"Peter, you can be an angel." She gave his arm a companionable squeeze. "We're using Cassidy's around the corner from the studio. Charlie Vargas, our director, is part owner and will be in charge of production."

"I'll be there at midnight." He stood up and winked at Vikki. "Mr. Falkner's all yours. Go get him, Vixen."

Vikki's bare feet hit the cold linoleum, giving a sobering effect to Peter's good-natured addendum: *Go get him, Vixen.* It wasn't Vixen who wanted Daniel Webster Falkner, it was Vikki, or was it? Good Lord, she had been weaving a crazy quilt of camouflage and coverup for so long that even she was confused!

What happened to that cautious, digni-fied, practical Capricorn personality that had ruled her life for thirty years? Why suddenly was she acting the part of the rambunctious goat, booting caution directly at its ruling planet, Saturn, and persistently and stubbornly ignoring common sense?

She knew why. The answer was standing across the room watching her every move-ment. She hadn't asked for Dan Falkner, she had never even prayed for someone like Dan Falkner, but such a man had been delivered. Wasn't there a post office rule that said you got to keep anything deliv-ered you didn't order?

Vikki fluffed out her hair and took a deep breath. Today's newspaper horoscope promoted her current feelings. *You've got the winning advantage and will discover hidden passion when a new relationship takes on another dimension.* A smile curved her lips. Who was she to cast aspersions on a set of astrology principles two thousand years old!

The lady warranted a moving violation. Dan hadn't realized just how hungry he was until his eyes were piqued by such a mobile feast of femininity. "I hope I didn't disturb your work."

Her fingers experienced the nubby wool weave on his brown and gray sports coat. "You always disturb me, Daniel, but I find it most pleasurable." Standing on tiptoes, Vikki planted a delicate kiss against the corner of his mouth. "Have you come to walk me back to the studio?" She stayed close against him, her emotions deriving sustenance from his warm body.

"I thought we could have lunch and continue with the interview." Dan sucked in a surprised breath when he discovered his hands luxuriating against a supple curve of satin flesh. "My deadline is Friday."

That makes two of us, she added in silent agreement. While her fingertips traced Dan's profile, Vikki reveled in the rough, masculine fingers that moved in caressing squiggles along her spine. *Oh, how I wish the two of us could have followed a soap-opera script to get to know each other. Our relation-*

ship would build and grow ever so slowly, note by cherished note, toward a mutually satisfying crescendo.

Vikki mentally slapped herself. Now she was viewing life through soap-stained glasses! Maybe the critics were right — too much illusion and fantasy could lead a person to believe reality was a television set.

"Does an invitation to lunch usually require such intense thought?"

Dan's chiding tone invaded Vikki's private musings. "I'm . . . I'm sorry, I didn't mean to drift away." Her lilting voice bridged the awkward silence. Vikki looked at the large studio clock and shook her head. "I have time for a fifteen-minute cup of coffee."

That wasn't good enough. Dan wanted more. "How about dinner? You owe me a raincheck."

"I know and I really want to, but my schedule is hellish today, Dan. I tape until ten tonight."

"We could make it a late supper. I'll cook."

Vikki stared at him in surprise. "Umm, I bet you can, but —" She was about to explain about the MADD commercials but remembered Vixen and thought better of

127

it. "I'm spoken for tonight." She turned away from Dan's sullen expression calling "Be back in a minute" and sprinted for the changing room.

Black wool trousers were pulled over red silk briefs and a hip-length black cardigan was buttoned and belted over the bandeau bra. Vikki hastily ran a brush through her hair, one side swept up in a black enamel comb behind an ear. Feet were jammed into black suede boots, the mink was slid on and her purse grabbed up by anxious hands. She didn't want to waste precious minutes that could better be spent with Dan.

"I didn't realize you were" — Dan hesitated slightly, choosing the words that would hurt him the least — "presently involved with someone."

Linking her arm into his as they jockeyed for a position on the snow-ridged sidewalk, Vikki hid a smile. "Did I say I was?"

"You *said* you were spoken for." His words exited in gray puffs that heated the frigid air.

"Just for tonight," she continued to tease, liking the reaction she was getting.

While Dan's expression was impassive, his voice exhibited anger. "You've got too

128

much class to be a one-night stand."

Vikki stopped in front of a coffee house. "Why, thank you, Daniel." She took pity on him but still decided to hedge her bet. "You're quite right, one-nighter's aren't my style." She freed her arm to open the restaurant door. "I know I couldn't have *just* one night with you." One blue eye winked in lusty appreciation. "I'm spoken for to do some extra filming, that's all. How about some coffee?"

Coffee turned into two cups of espresso served in glowing copper-cradled glass cups and a plate of butter cookies. Vikki savored everything — the aromatic brew, the rich pastries, and her delicious companion.

She was fascinated with Dan's every movement. She watched his long fingers pick up a spoon and proceed to create a whirlpool in the tiny cup. How well that depicted her own emotions — turbulent beneath a calm surface.

"Do I get a raincheck on your invitation to cook dinner?" Vikki inquired, relaxing in the cushioned bentwood chair.

"Maybe I should ask what your favorite food is to see if my rough skills as a chef would accommodate." Dan's upheld palm sought to block her immediate response.

"Let me take notes, I can use this is in the article."

When her laserlike stare failed to incinerate the fake-leather-covered notebook, Vikki set her tongue firmly against her cheek and went back to playing the risqué lead in their sensuous drama. "Favorite food . . ." Her tongue languorously washed russet lips; blue eyes turned into exotic slits. "Prime rib. I love sinking my teeth into rare aged beef."

Dan coughed, shifted uncomfortably and asked a much safer question. "Favorite song."

" 'Endless Love' and 'Let's Get Physical.' " Her voice dripped with innocence.

His pencil point broke; Dan reached for a pen and smiled. "Favorite holiday?"

"Christmas. I love bringing peace and good cheer to my fellow man."

Ink globs formed on the paper. "Favorite season?"

"Spring. Every year I indulge one young man's fancy and I love to watch the birds and bees cross-pollinate."

"You . . . uh . . . certainly give . . . uh . . . interesting answers," Dan reflected between sips of still steaming espresso. He'd thought the coffee would have cooled

130

to room temperature, but with Vikki the temperature in the room kept getting hotter.

Hands shoved inside her sweater pockets, Vikki viewed Dan Falkner with no trace of remorse. After all, what was there to feel guilty about? Every word she'd uttered had been the truth.

Rare prime rib was her favorite, although she'd just as easily feast on peanut butter and jelly. It wasn't *what* you ate, but *whom* you ate with that mattered.

"Endless Love" was one of her favorites, she owned both the single and the album. Olivia Newton-John's hit, "Let's Get Physical," was on the aerobics album she worked out to three times a week.

Christmas had always been special, more this year than ever before. Vikki's present had been airplane tickets bringing her four brothers, their wives, and fifteen assorted nieces and nephews to Connecticut for the holiday week. Her parents and grandparents had been thrilled to have everyone home for Yuletide.

What a celebration they'd had just two weeks ago. Ten perfect snowmen graced the yard, skates were rented at Rockefeller Center, Manhattan was shopped dry, and both her house and her parents' home were filled with delicious smells of home-made goodies. They had even thrown hot maple syrup on the new fallen snow, watching it turn into brittle. Christmas had never been better.

And yet spring had always been her favorite season and she did indulge one young man's fancy, her nephew, Todd, with birthday tickets to the Yankees' first game. She waited to see the first crocuses push through the slowly defrosting earth, stretching their purple blossoms toward the warm sun. Vikki even had a bird feeder but more often than not spent her time shooing squirrels and chipmunks out of the seed-ladened house.

"How about television?" A deep masculine voice broke her silent contemplation. "Do you have any favorite programs?" Dan watched a subtle change come over Vikki. Her posture was less relaxed, she sat at attention in the chair, her palms planted firmly on the white linen tablecloth.

"Besides *Always Tomorrow*, and courtesy of my video cassette recorder, I watch the other network soaps. The stories are expertly written and acted. Daytime beats prime time anytime."

"Of course, you're more than a little prejudiced," he countered smoothly.

"Me and thirty-five million other viewers."

"I'm not sure you can make an accurate judgment using housewives —"

One precisely defined eyebrow arched. "Did I hear a slight sneer in your voice?"

Dan blinked in confusion. "I — I beg your pardon?"

"Do you think *housewives* are incapable of making accurate judgments? Do you think *housewives* can interpret life only according to the gospel of the television set? That *housewives* need an on/off button to function?" Vikki drove home a very sharp probe.

The pen was thrown down; the gauntlet picked up. "Don't put words in my mouth, lady." Dan Falkner found his tone quite dogmatic. "I have the utmost respect for women who work in the home."

Blue eyes slanted in interest. "Do you?"

"Yes. I do." He enunciated each word carefully. "All women work, whether it's in a career situation or at home. In fact, I think it's safe to say women work harder then men. There seems to be an unwritten law that women have to prove themselves capable no matter what their qualifications or level of experience.

"My mother worked. Hell, my grandmother worked. They worked damn hard, both on the job and in the home." Dan's index finger punctured the air. "I was raised in one of the most democratic households you'd ever find. Nothing was labeled his and hers. Everything was ours.

"I'd come home from school and find my dad ironing; that didn't make him less a man. My job was starting dinner every night and setting the table. Sometimes my mother mowed the lawn. We had interchangeable roles; we supported one another. That's the way I still operate." Dan took a deep breath, opened his mouth, then closed it. He suddenly realized he had become the interviewee rather than the interviewer.

Vikki's low chuckle seemed to clear the air. "Well, Daniel, then you must go back and do a little more *investigative* research." Her mocking tone belied the respect that glinted in her eyes. "Housewives are only part of the daytime audience. College professors, factory workers, lawyers, doctors, politicians, actors all regularly watch soaps. It takes just one or two episodes to hook a viewer, after that they can't keep themselves from tuning in for entertainment, escapism, even education."

"Education?" His silver head shook in

disagreement. "I have a hard time believing that."

"Really?" Her tongue clicked against the roof of her mouth. "I am disappointed in your research. Shows have been done on juvenile diabetes, adoption, and numerous health problems. In fact, *Always Tomorrow* will be doing a story line on herpes. The writers and producers are waiting until summer to educate the young audience on where they can go for diagnosis and treatment."

Fingers flexing from his writing, Dan nodded in approval. "I stand corrected and I will dig a little deeper. Is it safe for me to say your favorite thing about soaps is the way they educate?"

She was thoughtful for a moment. "No, Dan, my favorite thing about soaps is the realistic way they portray women." Vikki smiled at his surprised expression. Of the thirty-one contract players on *Always Tomorrow*, eighteen are women. Only two are under twenty-one, eight are older than forty, and the rest are in their thirties. Every female character on the show works for a living. We have women doctors, not just nurses. As a matter of fact, one of our nurses is a man."

"How does that differ from prime time?"

"Prime time has given us T and A, jigglevision, and now the 'year of the hunk.' Prime time doesn't give either sex a compliment in the majority of cases and it shows in low ratings and audiences switching to cable.

"The success of any program is measured by how willing the viewer is to keep inviting the characters into their homes," Vikki reminded him. "Soaps get invited in day after day. The shows mirror human behavior, bring companionship, empathy, and humor — just like a family.

"We also bring women and minorities into the home the way they really are, not the way Madison Avenue depicts them. Women especially are reshaping society and controlling power. Prime time and movies see women over thirty as old while men get distinguished. We portray women as productive individuals into their seventies. Just the way it is in the real world," came her blunt reminder.

Dan knew he was listening to Victoria Kirkland rather than her alter ego. Now, however, he needed the addition of Vixen Mallory to get an accurate answer to his next question. "Don't you feel exploited? Don't you feel you're made to dress, act, and talk in an immoral sometimes amoral manner just to make sure viewers tune in and turn on every day?"

Oh, the man was so clever. And yet, Vikki found, she respected Dan for that. "Exploitation, like pornography, is in the eye of the beholder," she spoke from the heart. "Vixen's character is within the context of the show. Her personality is clearly and deliberately drawn so the viewers can see good versus evil. Vixen operates by her own rules. A set of values that she perceives is the truth."

Ice-blue eyes radiated a silent warning. "Be, advised, Dan Falkner, no one ever forces me to do anything I don't want to." Vikki slid her arms into her fur coat and stood up. "You never asked me to describe my favorite man." Her hand weighed heavily against Dan's shoulder, keeping him in the chair. "I'll tell you anyway, and then I have to go."

Her lips spoke warmly against his ear. "I like a sensitive, passionate man. One who knows when to be tender and when to be tough. He has to share and care, have a good sense of humor, and integrity. A man who won't mind if he doesn't always come out on top."

Vikki's fingers ruffled the silver-tipped black hair on his nape. "Rippling biceps and a macho swagger doesn't even jar my libido." Her hand moved along his shoulder. "But a wool tweed sports coat and spicy cologne definitely does." Even white teeth and determined lips sucked a love-bite into his neck. "Bye-bye, Daniel."

Another strong cup of espresso was required to sober Dan's nervous system. Inteviewing Victoria Kirkland was aging from the neck up and invigorating from the waist down. And in between? His fingers rubbed the bite below his ear. In between she could certainly activate the heart.

There was so much she wasn't telling him. Like that extra filming she was doing tonight. An inquisitive index finger tapped the closed notebook. Dan knew he wouldn't get a straight answer from anyone on the cast of *Always Tomorrow* — they were all thick as thieves. Maybe Peter Finch? Especially with the bribe of his name being mentioned in *Newsmaker* and using one of his photos!

CHAPTER SEVEN

A sense of discovery enveloped Cassidy's and Vikki suspected it was all due to the restaurant's ceiling. Suspended from rough-hewn beams, amid abundant copper-potted ferns, was a virtual museum of artifacts the owners collected from travels around the world. Ship's ornaments, airplane propellers, high-wheel bicycles, handicrafts, baskets, signs, and other novelty items added a rich ambience to the plank walls and stained-glass-enclosed booths that flanked a fifty-foot curved teak and brass bar.

Tonight people and cameras were added to the aesthetic ornaments that populated Cassidy's — a talented group that freely contributed their energies to wage war on drunk drivers. Vikki felt enormously proud that so many of her friends and coworkers had rallied to support a cause she so ardently promoted.

"Here you go, Vik, one turkey sandwich on whole wheat with mayo and a glass of club soda."

She gave the bartender a grateful smile

before staring in hungry passion at what was to be her only source of solid nourishment that day. And what a grueling day it had been!

Vikki thought back nineteen hours when she started at five A.M. with a morning heavy with rehearsals and scene blocking, the photo shoot with Peter Finch, then back to the studio for the final dress rehearsal and taping. Her teeth sank into a pickle and found it as sour as her afternoon. Camera four had gone down courtesy of a red deflection yoke, and videotape machine one lost its recording head, restricting the show to three cameras and three recorders. It had been a trauma to all involved.

Coffee and candy bars had stimulated Vikki with caffeine and sugar energy but now, at one A.M., more substantial fuel was needed to light her fire. Blue eyes stared at the beauty of thick white turkey liberally bathed with mayonnaise. She lifted half the sandwich to eager lips only to have sixty percent of it devoured by a blond mustachioed mouth.

"Peter!" Her hand beat against Finch's shoulder. "Order your own. I'm starving."

"That makes two of us, love," the photographer mumbled, reaching over her shoulder to confiscate the other half of the sandwich. "I haven't stopped all day. From here I go straight to a dawn shooting in Westchester." He caught sight of the barrel-chested director. "Charlie, where can I set up?"

Vikki grabbed Peter's arm, only to have her fingers skid along his white silk shirt. She watched in horror as her dinner almost disappeared in two giant bites. When she went to finish what was left, she was dismayed to find the bartender had swept the paper-plated remains into the garbage.

With her stomach welded to her backbone and her lower lip forming a pitiful moue, she slunk over to the director. "Charlie, do you have any more Snicker's bars?"

The bald-headed director looked at his half eaten candy bar. "Here, take the rest of this." Charlie ruffled her chestnut curls. "This does wonders for the digestion, heh, kid."

"Wonders!" came her tired rejoinder. Vikki was pulled onto a stool by the studio makeup man, who cluckingly plucked the candy from her fingers and devoured it himself before he worked his cosmetic wizardry on her face and hair.

Vikki played a mental game of escape and tried to tune out the chattering people and commotion of equipment for a temporary respite. Right this instant she felt a desperate need for a hot, suds-filled bathtub in which to submerge, her aching body and soothe her frazzled nerves. After which she'd cocoon herself in one of the homemade quilts that covered her brass bed, sip cocoa dotted with bobbing marshmallows, enjoy a crackling apple wood fire and soft music. A smiled curved newly crimsoned lips, such luxury!

Eyes forced closed by a shadow applicator, Vikki visualized the high point, of her day — coffee with Dan Falkner. How adept she was at recreating his image. In their own way, his easy smile, shaggy gray hair, and boyish features were also a luxury. She wondered where he was and what he was doing. Maybe he had decided to cook for some other woman. An added weight was levied on her shoulders that had nothing to do with overwork — just sorrow.

There was something startlingly sexy about décolletage that plunges toward a well-rounded derriere, Dan decided. His dark gaze traveled the supple curve of spine so temptingly displayed by Vikki's black velvet dress.

But when the actress stood to take her marked position for filming, he couldn't help but notice that the makeup man had been unable to totally conceal the shadows that haunted Vikki's usually electric eyes. There was a graceful weariness about her posture and movements; a fatigued expression masked her normally vital countenance.

Hands gripping the table, Dan had to force himself to remain seated, physically restrain himself from rushing across the room, sweeping Vikki off her feet, and carrying her away from all this confusion. He wanted to hold her, caress her, and make everything all better. Wanted? Dan rubbed an equally exhausted face with his hand. No, *needed*. Yes, he needed to show Vikki how much he cared. A caring that had little to do with sexual gratification.

A peremptory voice quickly changed a restaurant into a soundstage with "Quiet on the set. Get ready to roll." Dan did as he was instructed, looking toward the others for guidance in what to do once the filming began.

He watched in amazement the stunning transformation of Victoria Kirkland once the red light on the camera flashed on. Her previously enervated form became revitalized. Her voice and manner radiated sensual enticement that instantly captured and captivated all around her.

Dan found his respect for Vikki both as an actress and as a person deepening as the evening wore on. Her energy and spirit never lagged despite the fact that the filming lengthened into two hours and she was required to change clothes and hairstyles three times.

The slant and tone of the public service announcements, piqued his interest. Mothers Against Drunk Drivers, the American Automobile Association, the Salvation Army, and the National Institute of Alcohol Abuse and Alcoholism capitalized on the public's awareness of Vixen Mallory, television's leading female heartthrob. And Vixen didn't let them down.

While the public service spots varied in length from sixty, thirty, twenty, and ten seconds, they all fell victim to the provocative charm of daytime's reigning video vixen. Vikki played to the male ego in getting across the risk of too much alcohol, especially when you drive.

"It takes a real man to say no." Her sensual voice whispered seductively. "Oh, not to *me*." One blue eye winked into the camera. "Say no to one for the road and the rest of the guys. Remember the standard rule for staying sober is to drink no more than one ounce of alcohol, four ounces of wine, *or* twelve ounces of beer per hour. Nibble high-protein snacks like meat or cheese and dilute liquor with mixers and ice. If you overdo, allow time to sober up. Drinking coffee or taking a cold shower won't help. And don't drink if you are taking any medication. But, more importantly, if you drink don't drive. I like having you around."

After rewrites and retakes with ninety percent of the bogus restaurant patrons failing asleep on the tables, the camera crew yawning, and Vikki looking peaked despite the makeup man's best efforts, Dan was as thankful as everyone else to hear the director yell "Cut. I think we've got them all in the bag."

Charlie Vargas slid off a barstool and stretched flaccid muscles. "They look great, Vikki." His hands squeezed her bare shoulders. "You look ready to drop. It's been one helluva day, hasn't it?"

"Charlie" — her knuckles caressed his jowly cheeks — "I can't thank you and the crew enough for doing this. I — I —"

Words stumbled around the emotional lump that formed in her throat.

"Our pleasure, babe. Anytime." He looked at his watch and began barking orders. "Okay. Let's get packed up and out of here. We've got to be at the studio in five hours." A chorus of moans filled the otherwise companionable atmosphere. "All right, all right," Charlie laughed. "Seven hours and not a minute more."

Displaying the animation of a rag doll, Vikki let Peter Finch arrange her into the various poses he felt would make great posters. She somehow found the vivacity deep within hidden resources to look seductive on cue.

After saying good night to the hyperactive photographer, Vikki discovered the makeup man had packed her slacks, sweater, and boots in with the film wardrobe and taken them with him. A dejected figure stood in the center of the near empty restaurant clad in black satin pumps and a strapless black party dress, its skirt tiers of delicate lace.

"Can I be of service?"

Blue eyes widened at the sound of a familiar masculine voice, then closed in comfort when equally familiar hands curved their strength around her shoulders. "A silver-haired knight." Vikki relaxed against Dan's virile frame. "What would you do if I said I want to claim my raincheck for dinner right this minute?"

He spoke warmly into her ear. "I'd guide you into my yellow chariot, take you home, and cook you . . . breakfast."

"Perfect. Guide on, Dan Falkner." Vikki nearly collapsed when he helped her into her coat. This time the mink felt more like concrete!

The yellow chariot proved to be a taxi whose heater-warmed interior made Vikki's eyelids weigh more than her fur. "How did you find me?" She daintily yawned the question, her head resting comfortably against his broad cashmere-coated shoulder.

"As I recall, you were the one who suggested I use my investigative talents this afternoon," Dan chided in a low, tender voice. His fingers randomly played amid her vibrant brunette waves and became prisoners of luxurious curls. "You are totally exhausted. Don't you think tonight could have been postponed?"

The taxi's hiccuping stop-and-go movements jarred Vikki awake. "No." She blinked sleepily. "I was just thankful everyone's spare time meshed for the same night. All the work and use of equipment was donated. Despite the hour, the filming went beautifully."

Dan's thumb and forefinger captured her chin, lifting her face off his shoulder and up for inspection. "Tell me why you're so involved with this project. Fill me in on MADD."

Vikki was too groggy to be creative with any Vixenish lies. "Mothers Against Drunk Drivers are out to show people that it's not macho to drink and drive. Even modest drinking can impair a person's faculties, making them more confident. And that confidence in combination with an automobile can equal death."

She pushed his hand aside and once again sought the comfort of his shoulder. "Even with tougher laws and stiffer penalties people still climb behind the wheel under the influence. Figures and graphs, scare tactics" — she yawned — "none of it seemed to work. Now we decided to try a message sent on a glandular level and see if it registers."

He nodded, but his keen reporter's mind recorded the fact that she had explained MADD, yet hadn't answered his original question — what were her own personal reasons for becoming so involved?

Just then the scruffy-bearded cab driver rapped against the glass barricade. "That's two ten, Mac."

Dan shoved three dollars into the pay basket, opened the door, and, as gallantly as possible, hauled Vikki from the back seat. "You should be very glad I was able to get a co-op in this newer building." His tone was cheerful as he straightened out her coat and fluffed out her hair.

"Why's that?" Vikki inhaled a robust lungful of below-zero air, hoping Jack Frost's frigid artistry would make her more coherent.

He opened the glass front door and ushered her inside. "My old apartment was a fifth floor walk-up."

The oak-paneled elevator provided them with Musak to the eighth floor. Dan unlocked his apartment door, switched on the hall light, and jerked a thumb to the left. "The living room is that way. I'll just fix some food. . . ."

"Peanut butter and jelly would be fine." She gave him a weak smile.

"Cheese omelets, toast, and hot milk," he corrected, taking custody of the mink and her purse. His hand centered on the small of her back. "Go and rest."

Vikki went. Groping her way through murky unfamiliarity, she stumbled over an ottoman and fell backward onto the sofa. Soft plump cushions enveloped her in infinite comfort. Wet clammy shoes were kicked off; an elegantly clad body formed an exhausted curl on the couch.

Forty winks. A little catnap. Vikki yawned the silent promise. *I'll awake bright and charming and witty.* She snuggled her cheek against a tweed accent pillow. Her lips curved happily. The pillow smelled like Dan — rough and woodsy and decidedly male. Eyelids drifted closed courtesy of contented surroundings.

"Here we are." With practiced ease, Dan maneuvered around various furniture obstacles that loomed in the darkness. "Vikki, can you switch on a light. Vik? Ouch!" His shin had encountered the massive coffee table.

Dan cautiously set the food-ladened tray on the walnut surface and fumbled the end table's lamp into illumination. His dark gaze centered on the vixen who had turned into a sleeping kitten.

So many questions, answers, and emotions vied for resolution since he'd met Victoria Kirkland. Gentle knuckles traveled along her bare arm and shoulder to let careful fingers stroke back tumbled sable curls. The lady was a dichotomy, her every action a contradiction. Since he met her nothing had been the same.

Here was a woman whose very existence he had never imagined. For some reason she had destroyed his common sense, made his life an adventure, made him want to go out and conquer the world. Dan realized he wanted more than an interlude, he wanted to turn fantasy into reality, to stop searching and start hoping.

His silver head shook away his wants. He needed food. Good, hot, solid, substantial food. Dan quietly and swiftly appeased one of his appetites by eating both omelets, all four slices of buttered toast, and draining two glasses of warm milk. Then after stretching his satisfied but exhausted frame into the black leather recliner, he followed Vikki's example and fell asleep.

"Playing hopscotch at midnight on a restaurant's sidewalk is very silly."

"This is my last chance to be silly. I get married tomorrow. And doctors' wives are never silly."

"You stay and play another game. I'll go get the car." She could hear his laughter, it matched her own.

Suddenly she heard a screech, tires screaming against asphalt, then a thump, then metal crashing into metal. She blinked in amazement as one of the parking lot lights caved in. She followed the others who ran to see what happened. What she saw was —

A scream suddenly pierced the air. Dan fell out of his chair, scrambled on all fours to the couch, and grabbed Vikki. She was screaming, eyes closed, sitting bolt upright. Screaming, he thought, as if she had just seen death.

"Hey, Vik! Wake up, Vikki." He gripped her face, his fingers pulling away in surprise at the cold, clammy skin. "Vikki." Yelling her name and shaking her shoulders, Dan tried to vault this nightmare's barrier.

Blue eyes opened; lungs gasped for air. Vikki alternately pushed Dan away and clawed him closer, her mind tumbling in scared confusion. "What-what-what happened?" An ambulance, its siren wailing on the street below, made her hands tremble uncontrollably.

Masculine arms embraced her and sought to conquer her fear. "Take it easy. You're all right. I'm right here." Dan's deeply resonant voice soothed Vikki's anxiety while strong hands became tranquilizers that warmed and calmed her shivering body. "Everything's just fine." He could hear her breathing going back to normal and feel the tension ebb from her muscles.

Vikki clung tightly to Dan, his stability and strength soothing her ragged nerves. "I'm sorry. I — I —" She cleared her throat and leaned her head back. "I don't know what to say. . . . I should go."

"Do you really want to?"

"No." Her head rested on his shoulder, her face burrowed against his neck. Vikki had seen the compassion in his eyes and felt secure in the haven of his arms. "Apparently a screaming woman doesn't alarm any of your neighbors." Her fingertips tried to smooth the wrinkles out of his gray shirt.

"A screaming woman doesn't alarm *anyone* in Manhattan." Dan made his tone light to match hers. "Your mother should have told you to yell *fire*." His hands locked behind her waist. "Can I get you anything?"

"Just hold me."

"I intend to keep doing just that."

"What time is it?" She felt his hands move.

"Four thirty. You slept just an hour."

Only sixty minutes! How intricate and clever the brain. In that hour she had voyaged back a lifetime. Again her body suffused with exhaustion and her eyelids drifted closed.

Dan did what he had wanted to do earlier at Cassidy's; he picked her up in his arms and carried her off.

"I'm not going to have to yell *fire* am I?" Vikki smiled when the ear pressed against his chest filled with rumbled laughter.

"No. I just thought you'd be more comfortable sleeping in a bed." Balancing her on her bare feet, Dan flung aside bedspread, blankets, and a top sheet. "Don't get excited" — his fingers felt along the back of her dress for the zipper — "my intentions are purely honorable."

"I trust you." Despite her fatigue, Vikki realized she had spoken the truth. Her eyes intently focused on Dan's face, struggling to see his expression in the opaque grayness that cloaked the bedroom. "Stay with me, please."

"I intended to do that too." The delicate black lace dress was tossed in the direction of his valet. "Come on, let me tuck you in." His hand splayed against her back, fingers encountering satin feminine lingerie.

The sheets were cool against her damp skin. The blankets provided instant warmth, but Vikki discovered more tangible contentment in the arms of the man who now shared this bed.

"Sometimes it helps to talk about the bogeymen who terrify usually pleasant dreams." Dan's fingertips massaged gentle circles along her forehead.

"Curious?"

"Concerned."

Vikki was growing more relaxed by his tender ministrations. "I am so tired and so afraid to close my eyes. I haven't had this nightmare in three years."

His right hand sought hers, masculine fingers laced between feminine. "It has something to do with the drunk-driving spots you did tonight doesn't it?"

"What makes you say that?"

"I know it's not your work schedule, all though you really overdid it today." He spoke more harshly than he'd intended. "Process of elimination. You're too intelligent, too together to let something insignificant consume your courage — even when you're asleep."

She smiled at the compliment and squeezed his hand. "I'm more stubborn than courageous. Yes, that's the word."

Vikki yawned and curled herself close against Dan's side. "Stubborn, bullheaded, obstinate." Her hand moved across his shirt to settle over his heart. The steady, regular beat infused itself into her palm, into her very soul.

"Tell me about your dream."

"That's the trouble. It wasn't a dream. It was reality. I saw the deaths of two people."

"Two?"

"My fiancé and myself."

"No, you're alive," Dan told her fiercely, "you're here and very safe in my arms." Again he felt the tension invade Vikki's body and his hands expertly stroked it away. "Tell me what happened."

She was quiet for a moment, then suddenly felt the need to share this with Dan. Vikki cleared her throat, her voice oddly detached. "It was the night before my wedding, just after the rehearsal dinner at a small country inn in New Haven. A beautiful August night with a sky filled with diamond-bright stars and a moon that outshone the sun. I was being silly, playing hopscotch on the sidewalk while Gregg went to get the car.

"Then there were sounds, tires squealing, metal crunching and the entire restaurant ran out to see what had happened. I got there first and what I saw was Gregg. His body had become part of the car, mangled in the grill. His head was crushed — a bloody mass. He was dead. I could see it. I could smell it.

"The man inside the car was trying to get out, trying to kick open a door, but the lamppost he had skidded into jammed both of them. I watched him lean back in the front seat and lift a bottle to his lips and take another drink." Vikki didn't try to disguise her bitterness.

"The rest of the night was filled with sirens. Police. Ambulance. Fire department. The driver was arrested and released a day later on five thousand dollars bail. Five thousand dollars, that's all the judge thought Gregg was worth.

"What made things even worse was when we learned that the driver had three previous arrests for drunk driving and was driving under a suspended license. But the man knew someone, who knew someone, who owed someone a favor. Vehicular manslaughter and driving without a valid license was reduced because there was no implied malice and just being drunk wasn't enough to seek a murder conviction."

Dan felt the change in Vikki's skin. She

was cold and damp, and shivering. He pulled the blankets up around her shoulders and held her tighter. "So you've been working to change the system, to make new rules."

"Not just me, thousands of others. Thousands of angry, hurt people who have lost someone they love because of a drink and a car and a driver." She struggled to keep her eyes open, but the lids felt shadowed in lead.

"You said you died that night." His knuckles stroked her cheek.

"For the longest time I was dead. I was fueled by anger and hate. Anger at the man who killed my fiancé. Angry with the world because it thought so little of Gregg that it failed to punish his killer. Hating myself for grieving not only Gregg but the loss of my life, my future. Gregg's killer was free, but I was a prisoner of memories."

Dan experienced a rush of envy and had to choose his words with care. "Gregg . . . you must have loved him very much."

"Mentally, emotionally, spiritually, physically — all the ways to love. It was a long, slow process and he was so very patient with me." Vikki felt an increase in the rhythm of Dan's heart. "You were married. You must have known that kind of love."

"No, I'm sorry to say I didn't." His tone held a note of regret. "At eighteen I married the girl I had gone steady with since the tenth grade. The marriage was expected, a natural attrition after graduation. The novelty wore off quickly and we faced the reality of our youth, college, and employment. We grew, but in opposite directions. Two years later divorce seemed just as natural a progression. No tears, no regrets, just a heartfelt good-bye."

Her hand moved to his face; velvet knuckles caressed a beard-rough jaw line. "No memories?"

"Nothing that isn't relegated to the silliness and false maturity that is high school." Dan twisted closer, his legs insinuated themselves between hers. He silently cursed the material of his pants that barricaded him from her sleek, stocking-clad limbs.

"What about other women?" Her lips spoke against his mouth. "Hasn't anyone given you memories?" she inquired with sleepy curiosity. "A few scattered here and there." Dan's hands sought the luxury of feminine skin. Competent masculine fingers flowed warmly along her shoulders, collar bone and the velvety swells above the satin camisole. "Nothing that competes with the here and now."

Dan found he desperately wanted to erase the memories that haunted Vikki, erase the memories of another man. He tried to control the urgency that propelled his every movement. But it was a dominant male mouth that slanted hungrily over her half parted lips, stealing her breath, claiming it for his own.

His questing hands grew bolder and more tenacious as they sculpted the soft, generous curves of her breasts. His fingertip awakened a shy nipple, his thumb and forefinger proved erotic catalysts that teased it to erect delight.

Her low moans of pleasure fueled his ardor. His eager mouth branded possessive little lovebites along her neck and the curve of her shoulder. His tongue sampled her skin, enjoying the salty feminine dampness. The mysterious Oriental notes of her perfume played havoc with Dan's heightened senses.

His tongue made a slow circle of her breast, drawing closer and closer to let his teeth gently capture the pulsating peak. He enjoyed the feel of her hands pressing into his shoulder and back and the feminine fingers that tumbled his hair. Dan could feel Vikki's increased trembling against him.

It was her trembling that quelled his desire. He shook his head, cursing his self-ishness. His actions had been purely primitive and directed more at the memory of another man than the woman he now held in his arms.

"I'm sorry." Dan pulled Vikki close against him. "You should have yelled fire."

Her head moved softly in the curve of his neck. "I wasn't in any danger."

He felt the kiss against his throat. "Get some sleep." The regularity of Vikki's breathing came very quickly and although Dan's mind was in the same turmoil as his body, sleep was not as elusive as he had imagined.

The digital alarm on Dan's watch admirably performed its wake-up call at eight thirty. When he rolled over to check on Vikki, Dan found the bed empty.

Brown eyes blinked in amazement. Had he been the one dreaming last night? But when Dan buried his face in the other pillow the subtle nuance of Vikki's perfume assured him last night had been quite real.

CHAPTER EIGHT

Vikki had always considered a limousine the ultimate status symbol. One nice thing about using such luxurious transportation, however, was the fact you could double-park for hours in Manhattan and not get a ticket.

It even worked during rush hour on the Avenue of the Americas. Of course the chauffeur that came with the onyx automobile had a lot to do with the absence of the police. Vikki hoped Roderick's hulking form would have a more positive, persuasive effect on Daniel Webster Falkner.

Damn that man! Couldn't he keep his investigative nose out of trouble. All right, Vikki conceded, indirectly she may have instigated this little ruckus. She had suggested to Dan he should dig a little deeper into the scripts on the soaps. She just never thought he'd pick on Corinne Bradlee.

To say *Always Tomorrow*'s head writer was a basketcase was an understatement. Vikki remembered the phone call that jarred her lunch at her carriage house in

New Haven. "Falkner came in like a northeaster," Corinne had babbled. "He attacked me with one question after another. It was like an avalanche. Horrible! I couldn't breathe. I can't remember a thing I said. I'm scared. I have no idea what I told that man."

"For heaven's sake, Corinne, get ahold of yourself. You're getting excited over nothing. What could you have said that you're so worried about?"

"He asked me about our scripts, about the other writers, where we got our information, was there any personal experience involved. It seems *you* were the one who told him how educational we are. *You* were the one who told him to talk to the writers."

"I know Dan." Vikki had tried to calm her down. "I trust him. I don't think you have to worry."

"Sure, it's not *your* job that's on the chopping block. It's not *your* reputation. You come out smelling like a rose no matter how this project goes." Corinne all but sneered. "Damn it, what happened to one-for-all-and-all-for-one? I need help and you're the only one who can provide it."

"What the hell do you expect me to do,

Corinne? I can't turn back the clock. I can't give you back your words."

"Yes, you can, Vikki. He wrote everything down in his notebook. Get that for me. Let me see what I said. Then I'll have a chance. I can be prepared. I'll be safe. We've hatched a plan."

Blue eyes caught her grim reflection in the car's rearview mirror. Another great plan! The inside of her lower lip had been chewed raw ever since the group entered the world of scullduggery. Damn, if she didn't love them so much, if they didn't seem like part of her family, Vikki knew she'd have bailed out of this craziness before it had begun.

"We'd have better luck heisting the crown jewels than getting Dan Falkner's notebook," she had told the assembled company later that afternoon. But Vikki found every one of her objections had been systematically overruled.

So at seven o'clock on a below-zero January night, she sat in heater-warmed luxury, clothed in designer bait, with a key to an apartment she'd never seen before in her purse, lying in wait for Daniel Webster Falkner.

"Oh, what a tangled web we weave, when first we practice to deceive," Vikki mumbled, trying to relax into the sumptuous cranberry velvet upholstery. "Let's see how you get yourself out of this one, honey!" By the end of the evening it would be a miracle if she had any self-respect left at all.

Amazingly enough, her greatest concern was for Dan and what he'd think of her. Vikki was weary of this calculated façade, tired of being on guard and very, very bored with Vixen Mallory. Memories of last night had been replayed all day long.

Last night had been real and wonderful. Vikki had shared her true self with Dan and his response had filled her with joy. Here was a man who cared, a man with compassion. She had felt so safe and secure lying in his arms — so much a valued treasure.

Yet when her inner alarm clock had gone off at six thirty, Vikki had fled Dan's bed. She had left as though it didn't matter. Silver-shadowed eyelids blinked back burning tears. What a lie that was!

Dan Falkner managed to zigzag a course along sidewalks congested with equal parts of snow and people without ever lifting his gaze from the looseleaf binder. The pages made fascinating reading. They contained the latest audience demographics and photocopies of fan letters received by the cast of *Always Tomorrow*.

Despite the fact that millions of women abandoned daytime TV for careers of their own, the soap viewing audience got larger. In 1972 soaps had only five million viewers, now all three major networks and cable were cramming their daytime programming with soaps to satisfy the 55 million to 70 million Americans tuning in. Demographics showed the new soap devotees were young, affluent, and increasingly male. It seemed the male population were the ones writing the most fan letters — at least in the case of Vixen Mallory.

"Dear Vixen: Seeing you is the high point of my day"; "Vixen — You're so bad you're good!"; Dear Vixen: A day without you is like a day without sunshine." Dan agreed with that last sentiment wholeheartedly. Even with the weatherman's grinning prediction this morning, Dan had found his day very bleak indeed.

"Excuse me, sir."

"I gave at the office." Dan made the brusque pronouncement without raising his eyes from the binder. When further progress was halted, he looked up and continued to look up another twelve inches beyond his own six foot vantage point.

The stranger's shoulders seemed to go on for a city block; his neck appeared to be the same size as Dan's waist. "Of course, I suppose I could make another donation," Dan grinned, hoping his congenial manner would be reciprocated. The Falkners hadn't raised a fool!

"You're wanted, sir."

"Uh . . . well . . ." A white-gloved hand turned into a vise that gripped Dan's arm and pulled him toward a parked black limousine. When the uniformed chauffeur opened the rear door, a sassy-eyed, sultry-faced Victoria Kirkland was crooking one scarlet-tipped finger, inviting him inside.

"Good evening, Daniel. Tonight's the night to claim your raincheck for dinner." Noting his slight hesitation, Vikki added, "I told you yesterday I couldn't have just *one* night with you."

Despite the chauffeur's fist pressing into his spine, Dan had every intention of climbing aboard for what looked to be one hell of a bumpy ride. "Am I being shanghaied?"

Mink-coated arms formed a warm fur collar that encircled his neck. "Kidnapped for an evening of pleasure," ruby lips corrected before searing a silent sensual promise of future delights against his mouth.

Vixen-Vikki was back. Witty, confident, and devastatingly feminine. Dan became a joyous prisoner of nibbling lips and the enticing intrusion of her honeyed tongue. As always, she was compelling and vibrant and decidedly arousing. When she finally released his mouth, the very essence of Victoria lingered liked aged cognac.

With her fur-wrapped frame close against Dan's rugged body, Vikki concentrated on the pleasure of being with this man. How satisfied and complete she felt in his presence. There was nothing not to like about Dan, at least from her point of view.

Vikki liked his quick wit, emotional maturity, and even his tenacity where his career was concerned. Dan was more than just a handsome face. A lopsided smile curved her lips, although she wasn't going to deny the face, and body didn't go unnoticed.

Daniel Webster Falkner, the total man, ignited her mind and body like no one else. The first time she had fallen in love it had been so calm, so solid, so sensible — not this all-encompassing fire.

Love! Vikki swallowed convulsively. No,

that was impossible. She could not be in love. This was just . . . just . . . Vikki concentrated harder and realized she honestly didn't know just what this was!

Dan decided to break the intoxicating silence, not without a rather vigorous mental discussion on the topic. Last night still weighed heavily on his mind, as did Vikki's disappearance this morning, but he sensed this was not the time or place to ask any further questions. So he opted to discuss something they both had in common. "I've been visiting with Garner Broadcasting executives, sponsors, and your head writer today."

He reached for the red binder that had fallen on the car floor. "The latest demographics are even more impressive than the figures you quoted yesterday. I also talked to Corinne Bradlee about your educational scripts. I'm glad I took your suggestion to dig a little deeper. I found Corinne quite informative."

"Informative? Corinne?" Vikki winced and wondered what the writer did say. She cultivated a bored tone. "I find writers a tedious bunch to converse with." Her fingers walked along the arm of his cashmere topcoat until they came in contact with his chin. "Corinne, especially. The lady tends to babble on and on." A glossy fingernail rasped along his jaw, heading to torment an earlobe. "She tends to talk in two different directions at the same time. You almost need a script to follow her train of thought."

He stared at Vikki, the opera lights that illuminated the car gave her face an innocent ethereal glow. "Well, I will admit even with speed writing, I felt handicapped. The lady did ramble and talk in fragments." Dan patted his chest. "As a matter of fact, I was on my way back to the office to decipher and type all of my notes. The deadline for the article is tomorrow." His silver head nodded toward the curtained privacy window. "Your henchman certainly changed my plans."

"Roderick a henchman?" Vikki blew in his ear. "Why, he's a pussycat." Her tongue made tantalizing little thrusts into Dan's spice-scented ear.

"And where is this pussycat taking us for our evening of pleasure?" Dan inquired, being careful to sound more intrigued than amused. He was having a wonderful time and was anxious to sample the unexpected.

"I'm privy to a palace in the sky." Vikki looked past him, noting the nocturnal parade of lights and life had stopped. "I believe we have arrived."

There was something decidedly erotic about an apartment whose price tag was obviously in the six figures. Perhaps it was the wraparound balcony that provided a panoramic view of the East River and mid-town Manhattan, or the numerous skylights that rendered the feeling of being at one with the universe, or the thirty-foot living room's sumptuous decor.

Probably the most erotic appointment in this fabulous penthouse, Dan decided with his hand shielding an appreciative grin, was the tall, chestnut-haired woman who smoldered below-surface mystique. A woman whose voluptuous figure shimmered beneath a column of liquid midnight that flowed from a draped silk knot on a single shoulder.

"Well, Daniel, what do you think?" Vikki stood in the center of the living room, slender arms making a graceful sweep that encompassed the elegant pale-blue furnishings.

"Stunning." His dark eyes stalked the rounded feminine proportions hinted at beneath the narrow crepe. "And this place isn't too bad either." Her throaty laugh stimulated a more primitive arousal than

Dan had anticipated.

Vikki slithered against him, her breasts and pelvis branding a womanly impression into his tan suit. Her hands flattened. along the lapels, her right palm stumbling over the ridge of his notebook. "Why don't I make you a little more comfortable." Her fingers wiggled apart the buttons on his jacket. She had tried to take off the suit jacket when she had hung up his winter coat but found that task impossible.

Dan decided to play hard-to-get. "Actually I'm a little chilly." Masculine fingers stopped their feminine counterpart's attack. "I'll just keep the jacket on until I get warmed up."

Guileless blue eyes scrutinized the enigmatic face inches from her own. "Let me raise your thermostat, Daniel," Vikki offered. Fingers filtering through his hair, she forced his head down to meet hers.

Her teeth nibbled satin bites into his lower lip; her tongue darted a tantalizing, ever deepening path into the lush cavern beyond. Vikki felt Dan's arms wrap around her torso, his hands spread like warm fans across her back and spine.

The intimacies shared by mouths and tongues proved a heady stimulant to her feminine psyche. Each encounter with this man became more emotionally rewarding, more physically exciting. Vikki's fingertips moved with deliberate slowness along the underside of his jaw and along his neck. She found his rapidly beating pulse matched the thunderous pounding of her own heart.

With a low groan Dan pulled his mouth free. "You can certainly raise a man's body heat." Male intuition signaled that Vikki was up to something, but Dan was perfectly content to participate in whatever illusion the lady decided to create. He wouldn't destroy tonight's magic.

"Come" — she took possession of his hand — "I've prepared a tempting array of canapes to pique your appetite." Vikki followed the pale-blue carpeting into the dining room.

She saw that the perpetrators of this elaborate ruse had been hard at work. There, in the windowed alcove, with the moon and stars the only sources of light, an intimate table had been set for two. The glass top reflected fragile crystal goblets, pristine white china, and three bottles of champagne in ice-filled buckets.

Dan squinted at the labels, his dark brow arching in pleasure at the ten-year-old blanc de blancs. "You've certainly outdone yourself."

"Sit down, Daniel." Vikki all but pushed him into the delicate Oriental-style dining chair. "It will be my *pleasure* to serve you." Her knuckles skimmed along his jaw before she moved to a nearby brass serving cart.

Dan was finding it very difficult to keep a straight face. While her manners were erotically impeccable, he wondered how long it would be before this subservient attitude choked her. This was quite a change of pace from her normally aggressive stance.

"Here we are." With more flourish than necessary, Vikki centered a silver serving dish on the small table, then she pulled her own chair next to Dan's.

"Uh . . . it . . . uh . . . certainly is an interesting assortment." He stared at the tray, then at Vikki in puzzled contemplation. Had she abandoned Vixen Mallory in favor of Lucrezia Borgia?

Black velvet lashes fluttered an enticing silent message. "Daniel, I thought we could do more than just pique our food appetite. I thought we could excite our sexual appetites as well."

Vikki's smile was as guileless as her eyes.

"This is a romantic little dish perfect to warm a frosty night." Her fork speared the first aphrodisiac. "Try a wine-soaked chestnut." She popped the inspirational Chinese delicacy into his mouth.

"Good?" She smiled at his humming nod. "A little caviar on a slice of cucumber." She was delighted to watch her offer so readily consumed.

"And this, Daniel." Vikki abandoned the fork to use her fingers. "Strawberries." She dipped the giant ruby-red fruit into powdered sugar. "They were Venus, the goddess of love's, favorite." Watching his even white teeth sink into the juice-filled berry, her fingers became teasing little napkins that blotted the sweet nectar from his chin and transferred it to her mouth.

"Ummm. While I get the champagne" — she stood, her hand squeezed his arm — "why don't you have some oysters? You're going to need the extra stamina." Quickly turning away, Vikki pretended inordinate interest in the wine bottles and hoped the expensive vintage would wash away the sour taste that tainted her mouth.

Vikki took a deep breath and tried to banish the wave of repugnance she felt for herself. *This is the home stretch,* came her silent directive, *only this one last thing left to do.* The champagne bottle wrapped in white linen, she turned a composed, smiling face back to Dan.

He returned the smile. "Would you like me to open that? Those high-pressure corks can be tricky."

"No. No." The bottle was quickly lifted out of reach. "As a matter of fact, it's already loosened. See." Her thumbs released the cork. While the projectile was aimed into safety, the previously agitated wine gave an Emmy-winning performance in the role of Mount Vesuvius, erupting and burying its victim in frothing fury.

"Oh, Daniel. How dreadful." Reaching for a napkin, Vikki proceeded to finish emptying the bottle over his entire suit. "Oh, I can't believe I'm so clumsy."

"Neither can I." He grabbed the linen from her hand, but the small square of fabric proved quite ineffectual in soaking up a magnum of liquid.

"Why don't you go into the bedroom and get out of these wet things. The wine is awfully sticky." Her hands brushed together. "While you take a shower I'll use my hair dryer on your jacket and pants." Vikki gave Dan another winning smile. "You'll be as good as new in no time."

Despite his mumbled protests, she led

him back through the living room to the magnificently appointed master bedroom. "There's towels in the bathroom and I think my robe is in there too." Vikki helped him out of his jacket.

Dan gave her an inquisitive look; he found himself very confused with this sudden change of events. Perhaps it was an accident. He handed her his tie and unbuttoned a soggy shirt. "Don't you think your robe will be a bit small?"

"Then you'll have a good excuse to take it off!" She pressed a moist kiss to his half opened mouth. "Don't take too long, Daniel, we still have the entrée and a very special dessert."

CHAPTER NINE

Vikki sat on the edge of the massive plat-
form bed and stared at the spoils of victory:
Dan's notebook. This brown-leather-covered
pad was the coveted prize — a prize won by
more foul means than fair.

Now she had to execute the dénoue-
ment. Vikki was supposed to take not only
the notebook but Dan's clothes, leaving
him with just a towel and a bathrobe in a
furnished model penthouse where the telephone was just another phony prop. The
"last laugh," as her castmates viewed it.
Roderick would deliver Dan's suit
tomorrow morning. And what man would
be stupid enough to vent anger on a chauffeur built like King Kong!

That was the plan. A plan Vikki thought
bordered on insanity and she had said so.
This afternoon her TV family had spent
hours contradicting her every argument
and bolstering her waning enthusiasm by
suggesting she disassociate Victoria Kirkland from the project.

Was she not, after all, a "natural

actress"? Become Mata Hari for the evening, pretend this was nothing more than a scene from a spy movie. Vikki had psyched herself up to do just that. It had almost worked. But like Mata Hari she had lost sight of her original motives and succumbed to a greater force.

As an actress she expressed outward emotions, unlike people who kept their emotions inside. But right now, right this minute, Vikki was no longer an actress playing a part. She was a woman with tremendous feelings. Deep inside, trust, loyalty, love, obligation and stupidity were all at war.

Pushing herself off the bed, Vikki walked across to the wall of windows. Manhattan shone like a necklace dazzled with ruby, sapphire, emerald, and diamond lights. How calm, serene, and untroubled the city looked. A wry smile curved her lips; it seemed she was a falsehood surrounded by illusions.

She rested her forehead against the cool glass. Right and wrong used to be so simple. She longed for the time when her life was filled with absolutes — black and white — not this confused mass of gray.

No matter what, she'd end up a loser. Vikki took a deep breath and came to a decision. She wouldn't tarnish this evening with any more deceit. Her feelings for Dan were real and needed to be acknowledged.

The notebook was returned to the safety of the inside jacket pocket and the suit was neatly folded on an accent chair. Trust had won. So had love. Possibly stupidity. But not in Vikki's viewpoint. For once her heart and her head were totally synchronized. Whatever happened after tonight — be it losing Dan, her job, or her friends — she'd have no regrets. She had herself to contend with. When the bathroom door opened Vikki knew everything would be all right.

"How did the suit come out?"

She walked toward the masculine figure cloaked in bathtowels and wreathed in steam. "I decided to let it air dry." Her hands grasped the edges of the white towel slung around his neck. "I'm afraid it will take all night."

Dan stared at Vikki. In the celestial shadows that filtered the darkness, she seemed like a gossamer phantasma. "Your robe was too small." He wasn't sure why he mumbled such an inane comment.

"That just saves me the trouble of removing it." Her left hand spread across his chest while her right hand pulled away the towel around his neck and dropped it onto the rug.

"Do you know what you're doing?" His voice was hoarse and demanding.

"I like to think so, Dan." Her luminous eyes claimed his. "But if I do anything you don't like, just let me know."

Palms pressed into his shower-damp flesh, Vikki's fingers turned into provocative envoys that played amid the swirls of thick dark hair that covered his torso. Her lips left their imprint along his collar bone, delicate kisses that inspired a guttural sound of pleasure.

"Victoria, this is your last chance to stop if you're just teasing." Strong masculine hands clamped tightly at her waist, alternately holding her off then bringing her closer.

The scent of soap and clean male skin tantalized her nose, proving more of an aphrodisiac than any manufactured cologne. "I'm not teasing." Her teeth sucked another live bite into his neck. "Well, maybe just a little." Her tongue licked away the erotic sting.

"My intentions are purely honorable." She ignored Dan's eager lips to bestow light kisses on his throat, chin, and jaw. "I intend to seduce you." Her warm breath tantalized his ear. "I intend to explore and enjoy every inch of your body."

Vikki's enticing kisses and baiting words of promise had piqued her own appetite. She consumed his anxious mouth with an unrestrained hunger of her own. Dual moans of delight were the only sounds that interrupted the intoxicating silence. Her tongue again found its mate and enjoyed a glorious reunion inside his welcoming mouth.

She wanted this moment to last forever. She lost all her inhibitions in Dan's arms. In giving him pleasure she experienced a corresponding enhancement of her own sensuality, a heightened awareness of what it was to be a woman that she had never before experienced.

"Oh, God, you're driving me crazy," Dan growled, burying his face in the fragrant wealth of her hair. Jasmine and roses embraced his senses, heightening them like a drug. He swayed slightly, his arms trapping her firmly against him.

"I haven't even started yet," she whispered with insouciant boldness. Her hands traveled the muscled landscape of his shoulders and back, fingernails scraping erotic little patterns along his spine. When Vikki encountered terry cloth instead of tough masculine flesh, she quickly disposed of the obstructing towel.

Dan's hand moved along her slender arm and shoulder. "You've given me an unfair advantage." His silver head nuzzled along her neck while competent fingers untied the crepe knot that was the sole support of her gown.

Hands still around his waist, Vikki took a half step back, the silk dress shimmered to the carpet. Her bare feet kicked it to one side and with it went all her old inhibitions. She felt confident in her own sexuality and the look on Dan's face further confirmed her allure.

"You are even more beautiful than I imagined." His eyes devoured her full but lithe body. "And my imagination was running quite wild at times." Roughly he pulled her into his arms. "I love the way you feel against me."

Vikki purred in response to the firm masculine hands that stroked her spine. The rhythmic mastery of his touch sent waves of erotic electricity into the very essence of her femininity. She felt warm and safe and secure.

She peppered his chest with buttery-soft kisses. "Didn't I promise you a massage?" Hand in hand, they moved to the king-size bed. "Is it proper to tell a man he has a beautiful body?" Her chestnut hair moved sinuously across his back as she whispered into his ear, "You do, you know."

Her hands pampered his virile length, fingertips pressed into the sinewy bands that transversed his broad shoulders. Her palms made ever windening circles as they massaged his taut muscles, her full breasts contributing to the sexy soothing.

"You're making it increasingly difficult for me to lie on my stomach," Dan murmured, his tone reflecting satisfied discomfort. Her throaty laugh bubbled into his ear. "Mind if I turn over?"

Vikki let her fingertips brush up and down the length of his torso ever so lightly. The feathery massage just barely touched Dan's skin, making him tingle from scalp to toe. She indulged herself with another kiss, enjoying the sustenance his mouth and tongue provided.

Her lips and tongue moved on, anxious to sample further delights on his masculine anatomy. She nuzzled the inside of his elbows; lips tasted the rubbery toughness of his nipples; her tongue danced in spirals along his bottom rib. "I see you possess both an innie" — she kissed his navel — "and quite an outtie," and her fingers moved to delicately caress and explore his engorged male spirit.

Dan gave a low groan, luxuriating in the supreme pleasure her hands and mouth bestowed. Her hair moved like silk across his pelvis as I soft moist kisses tantalized his inner thigh.

Vikki was intoxicated by the power she had over Dan. His whispered words of pleasure sparked her own desires, inciting tiny eruptions that brought her to exquisite arousal.

Her breasts foraged through the dark hair on his thighs, stroked his flat stomach and chest. Her graceful feline form absorbed his naked length, the essence of her femininity coveted and consumed his intrinsic maleness.

She felt complete in this beautiful intrusion, her body naturally setting the rhythm of shared desire. Vikki concentrated on this mutual sweetness but found her own sensibilities heightened beyond her wildest expectations.

Dan's hands moved from controlling her hips to span her waist and suddenly toss her down on the satin bed cover. "Victoria, love, you've finally given your true self," his deep voice rasped into her ear. "While I enjoyed your going first, I insist on being the last."

The inference of his remark was lost amid Vikki's passion-drunk senses. Her hands gripped his head, pulling his mouth down to hers. His hard tongue proved to be the missile that intercept her half parted lips. She groaned in pleasure and acquiesced to his erotic commandeering of her body.

His hands sculpted her lush form, his lips burning a trail of heated kisses across her breasts. His tongue drew delicate patterns around the nipples, bringing the peaks to taut fullness under the gentle ministerings of his teeth.

Vikki was alternately pleasured and tormented by his hungry caresses. Her lower body burrowed a silent invitation to again possess him. Her fingers walked a titillating trail down his stomach and across his hips to press another urgent message into his buttocks.

Dan's mouth reluctantly freed a suckled nipple, planted warm, eager kisses along her ribs and against the scented skin of her rounded belly. He found her navel, his tongue sculpted the perfect circle, and then moved lower, bathing her body in sensuous dampness, seeking the enticing intimacy that made her a woman.

She shuddered against the exquisite little

quakes that ravished her body and moaned in delicious abandon as Dan discovered all the erotic little nooks and crannies that were meant to enhance pleasure.

His face filled her eyes, his hands lifted her hips to receive his thrusting desire. His virile potency filled her completely. Two became one under the dynamics of a wondrous and joyful union.

Her long sleek legs embraced his powerful hips. She luxuriated in his every stroke, her own ardor increased as he grew stronger and deeper. His lovemaking was vital and forceful.

Vikki's body was awash with surges of passion that brought her closer and closer to the peak of ecstasy. Her body vibrated around him, synchronizing her own rhythmic movements with his. She felt her inward sensations exploding out of control.

She pulled his head down, her trembling mouth needing the security of his firm lips. Inner fireworks exploded. Her fingernails clawed into Dan's flesh as her body jolted under a series of distinct, shattering pulsations.

His hands brought her even tighter against him. In three quick thrusts his own body erupted in a beautiful effusion deep inside of her. Trembling with the intensity of his emotions, he collapsed on top of her, his face burrowed in the curve of her neck.

Locked in each other's arms, they were both deliciously at peace in the culmination of their love. For Vikki the feeling of intimacy was so overwhelming her eyelids blinked rapidly, trying to banish the tears that formed.

"You are everything I ever wanted." Dan kissed her forehead, her nose, and finally her lips. "Everything I ever dreamed," came his husky words of worship.

Vikki snuggled close against his heated flesh, an ear resting above his heart. She smiled at the intense pounding, echoing her own splendid arousal. Her lips savored with new delight the salty taste of his shoulder. *I love you.* The words were spoken silently, both in heart and mind. Vikki found her courage had deserted her; she now felt more vulnerable than ever.

She banished all thought of future recriminations and concentrated on the present. Cuddling close into him, her toes wiggled a suggestive trail along his calves, over the tops of his feet, and on his soles. Silken legs slithered intimately between his athletic thighs, her softly rounded belly pressed into his flat stomach.

"You're very quiet." His hands sculpted the lush contours of her body, reveling this possession. "I didn't hurt you, did I? I wouldn't, Vikki. You must know that."

Her fingers stilled his lips. "I'm fine. Wonderful. I'm just enjoying you, enjoying our time together." Her mouth replaced her hand, uniting with his in fervent emotion.

Vikki knew the love and closeness that took shape in the magic of tonight would permeate her life. In the afterglow of a loving ambience, she closed her eyes and committed to memory their torrid passion.

Precisely at eight A.M., the alarm watch once more did its duty. When Dan blinked into full alertness he again found himself alone. The penthouse was inordinately neat and tidy, as though everything had been a dream.

CHAPTER TEN

Vikki decided the weather suited her mood perfectly. The mercury had frozen at thirty-two and thick, black-bellied clouds grouped the sky in threatening formation. Lungfuls of cold air had little effect on her body. Why should it? She had been numb for the last twenty-four hours and the grimness of her surroundings only echoed the bleakness in her heart.

Looking back over her shoulder, Vikki stared at the giant footprints her furry Eskimo mukluks had left in the snow. The pristine virgin beauty had been destroyed by her shuffling boots. She sighed and shook her earmuffed head. She had certainly cornered the market on destruction. Yesterday it had been friendships!

Silver-fingered dawn was splitting the Friday morning sky when she arrived at Corinne Bradlee's apartment — without Dan's notebook. Her reception was not unlike Mata Hari's. Instead of a French firing squad, Vikki fell victim to a verbal barrage.

Her castmates had been livid. Under an onslaught of insults and tearfully flung aspersions, Vikki finally dug in her heels. "I think you've all gone crazy," she'd yelled at Noel, Peter, Heather, Jerry, and Corinne. "Dan's not going to murder us. Sure he's asked some pointed, hard-hitting questions, but that's the nature of his business.

"We did our best to show him how difficult our work is. We answered his every attack and countered with our own kudos. *Newsmaker* magazine is not about to alienate fifty-five million soap-opera fans by printing a derogatory and possibly slanderous article."

Jerry's lips curled, his tone rude. "Aren't you forgetting that it was just such an article in that magazine that got us to this very point?"

"Fear got us to this point," Vikki countered. "Fear and irrational anger. We're our own enemies. Dan Falkner is not a vindictive person. But, by God, he'd have reason to be if I acted out your scenario last night! I trust Dan. I thought you all trusted me." But her pleading words fell on deaf, or, more correctly, scared ears.

After exhaustive arguing and trying to quell lacerated nerves, Vikki realized she was accomplishing nothing. She returned to her carriage house feeling like a leper. From Daniel Webster Falkner she heard nothing. So she crawled into bed, pulled her two handmade quilts over her head, and wondered what would happen next!

The raucous cry of a crow that had stubbornly refused to spend the winter in Florida brought Vikki back to the present. Under the wary scrutiny of two gray squirrels, she hung the last of the suet and birdseed balls on the sweep bough of a blue spruce, the last evergreen in a windbreak curve that edged her property.

In the distance, surrounded by towering pines and barren maple trees, stood her barnboard-sided carriage house. Snow had rendered added charm, making the two-story structure look like it should grace the front of a Christmas card.

Last year Vikki had traded the hustle-bustle of Manhattan for the woodsy beauty and privacy of Guilford, Connecticut. The entire township, including the rural areas, boasted a population slightly over twelve thousand. The only intruders were tourists taking pictures of the Whitfield House, built in 1639 and reputed to be the oldest stone house in New England.

She love the responsibility of a house

and grounds and had become quite proficient in making minor repairs to the plumbing and heating systems. Vikki had done all the painting and wallpapering, and had sewn most of the curtains. A mixture of antique and contempory pieces, the furniture was comfortably eclectic. In the spring she planted a garden and for Christmas Vikki had purchased a riding lawnmower with a snowplow attachment that now shared garage space with her Toyota.

Lately, however, her workday often stretched past ten P.M. and the seventy-mile trip home seemed like an odyssey. *Always Tomorrow*'s viewers were demanding to see more of Vixen Mallory and Vikki's scenes had been expanded. Courtesy of her producers, she often stayed at the Barbizon Hotel.

A wry smile twisted her lips. Vikki guessed she would have lots of free time shortly. Yesterday Corinne had mumbled something about giving Vixen a disease. And in the world of soaps a disease was the kiss of death for an actor or actress!

Two snowpeople, left from the Kirkland family Christmas sculpting session, stood guard over her backyard. Vikki patted fresh snow into the rounded bodies, straightened old hats and scarves, and repositioned woodchips that served as eyes, noses, and mouths.

She stepped back and surveyed her handiwork. "He's really quite handsome," Vikki told the smaller snowlady. "At least you know where he is and what he's doing." She didn't have the luxury of that knowledge about Dan. The wind picked up, making her shiver despite the goosedown lining of her snowmobile suit. Vikki tramped the snow from her boots as she followed the shoveled path to her back kitchen door.

The black snowsuit, boots, mittens, and earmuffs were hung on various hooks in the mudroom. Clad in red thermal shirt and pants, Vikki tried to decide what would be more soothing, a hot bubble bath or a cup of tea and stoking the fireplace with apple wood.

The bath would wash away all traces of Dan. Vikki knew she was acting like a silly teenager, but she didn't want to cleanse away his memory. No matter what the final outcome of these past weeks, she didn't regret her actions. She didn't regret her night of love. Hands fluffing out her matted chestnut curls, she opted for the tea.

The kitchen was filled with the fresh smell of gingerbread. Vikki's hand automatically went toward the plate of dark, spice-rich squares. Whenever she was depressed or confused, she baked. Unfortunately she also ate. Six pieces! She swallowed number seven and resolved to double up on the aerobics this week to work off all the calories.

A loud hiss, a sharp pop, and a crack made her turn off the faucet, put down the teapot, and look through the open counter area into the living room. The stone hearth held a bonfire behind the drawn metal protection screen and the tempered glass doors stood open. Vikki's forehead puckered in silent contemplation; she distinctly remembered spreading the ashes and closing the doors before going on her walk.

A movement on the arm of her beige-and-brown tweed sofa caught her eye. Two feet in dark socks were waving a greeting. She ran around the counter partition and found the feet were the property of: "Dan!"

"You are a tough lady to track down." An easy grin spread across his mouth. "Unlisted phone number, castmates who are clams. When I finally appease your cohorts in crime and they give me your address, I have to rent a jeep to find this charming place in the middle of the woods."

"What . . . how . . . why . . ." Vikki stopped, took a deep breath, and tried to marshal more coherent thoughts.

"You have one very bad habit that I intend to break this weekend." His arm was a swift messenger, delivering a hand that gripped the front of Vikki's shirt and pulled her onto his chest.

"Really?" Blue eyes narrowed in humorous contemplation of his grinning features. Vikki was alive again, every fiber of her being crackled with loving electricity. "And what bad habit is that, Mr. Falkner?" Her officious inquiry belied the feminine body that sought an intimate alignment against his virile frame.

Dan's fingers captured her chin, lowering her lips to his. "The fact you keep disappearing out of my bed. I figure by Monday morning at the latest you'll be so thoroughly entranced with my love-making you won't ever want to escape."

"Is this a proposal or proposition?"

His tongue tantalized the corners of her lips. "Oh, I'm betting *you'll* propose."

"Me?" Vikki tried to sound indignant. "Now, why should I do that?" Her legs slid with suggestive intent between his tan-corduroy-covered thighs; her bare toes nuzzled the soles of his feet.

The serious expression in Dan's eyes echoed the one on his face. "Because you love me." His arms wrapped around Vikki, making her a prisoner. "Maybe not quite as much as I love you. But enough to make you *not* steal my notebook.'" At her indrawn breath his tone became quite gentle. "You love me enough to give yourself. Completely and freely with no questions and no strings. And I know you well enough, Victoria Kirkland, that you couldn't have done it if you weren't in love."

"Ohhh, you are such a smart man!" Her smile was consumed by his hungry mouth. Vikki felt at once content and complete. Her tongue lightly teased his, knowing with delight this same pleasure would be hers forever. Reluctantly she freed her mouth, needing it for some clarifying words. "So now you know about the plot to steal the notebook."

"I wasn't quite the fool I pretended to be Thursday night." His index finger tapped her nose. "I knew you were up to something, but I couldn't figure out what, so I opened the bathroom door and peeked."

197

Vikki winced and looked away, concentrating her attention on the colorfully burning firelogs. "This . . . this whole thing started out as revenge for that first article in *Newsmaker*. And I was the" — her gaze meshed with his — "scarlet herring. Only we were prepared to gaslight Kip Hallen and when you arrived, with *investigative reporter* engraved on your business card, we thought the magazine was out to do us in."

"So you all decided to do unto others *before* they do unto you, is that it?"

She nodded. "Something like that." Her fingertips pressed lovingly into the planes and angles of his face. "You know, Dan, you certainly fired some damnable questions at me!"

He chose his words with care. "They were questions that needed your side to make more definitive answers. But I had a selfish reason too," Dan announced with a rueful grin. "It was then that I was able to talk to Victoria Kirkland rather than Vixen Mallory. Vikki provided the meat and Vixen the spice."

Reaching over his head, his fingers felt for the sheaf of papers on the oak end table. "I brought the article with me. It's not all champagne and roses, but your castmates, your producers, and your publicity department were thrilled. Corinne Bradlee said to tell you vixen would remain healthy."

"Well, at least I'm still employed." She laughed but her own hand halted his. "I don't need to read it, Dan. I knew all along your story would be accurate and fair. I trust you."

Again his mouth took possession of hers, his hands slid beneath her shirt, stroking her silken skin. "Vikki" — Dan rested his forehead against hers — "why such an elaborate ruse? What the devil was everyone so scared an investigative reporter would uncover?"

Vikki took a deep breath. "I'm sorry." She pressed a gentle kiss to his lips. "They aren't my secrets to tell."

"I'll respect that. What about you? Do you have any secrets?"

She rubbed her head along the curve of his neck, a satisfied purr coming from her throat. "Only the one you already discovered." Vikki's fingers unbuttoned his gold plaid flannel shirt; her hands pushed aside the brushed cotton to splay across his warm flesh. She peppered his chest with quick kisses. "I love you very much." Blue eyes slanted in vixenish delight. "When did you fall in love with me?"

He began to unsnap the front of her shirt. "I became fascinated with your pictures in *Playboy*; your clothed body proved more stimulating than the centerfold." Dan grinned as he effortlessly undressed her. "Of course I find your unclothed body quite intoxicating also." Her bra followed her shirt to the floor.

"I happen to be a student not of Will Rogers" — one brown eye winked at Vikki — "but of Oscar Wilde. I too am satisfied only with the best and I can resist everything but temptation. You, Victoria, provide both." Dan luxuriated in the feel of her satiny breasts pressed into his hair-rough torso.

Lifting her chin, he stared deep into her eyes. "I know it's happened fast. But I am very, very positive about my feelings for you." Dan caught his bottom lip before continuing. "I also have to tell you how much I envy what you had with your fiancé. Your love must be very great if you still have those dreams."

Vikki cradled his face between her hands. "Dan, my dreams are not about love . . . just the nightmare of a horrible accident that I see duplicated almost every day on the front page of the newspaper.

"As far as my relationship with Gregg, I

was twenty-two when we met and a very late bloomer. He was vey patient, very kind, and very loving. He believed in me when I was consumed with uncertainty."

Her lips curved into a tender smile. "Funny thing, it took me a long time to share myself physically with a man I was going to marry. And even then it wasn't total; it wasn't as complete and abandoned as my love for you." Vikki teasingly avoided his seeking lips.

"You, Daniel Webster Falkner, just kept creeping up on me. I looked forward to seeing you every day, of having our intimate verbal battles." She gave him her best leer. "Ninety percent of the time I was not being Vixen Mallory. I was me and dreaming day and night of making love to you in the most thorough manner."

Sliding sideways against the back cushions, Vikki let her hands explore his sinewed strength. Her fingers deftly unbuckled his belt, releasing the hook and the zipper that held his slacks. She found herself trembling at the magnificence of his masculine beauty. Vikki looked at Dan. "Do you know how hard it was for me to leave your bed? To walk away from the man I loved as if the night we spent in each other's arms didn't matter?"

With a hungry growl he pulled her beneath him. "I love you, Victoria." He adorned her face with kisses; his lips moved down the slim column of her throat to her breasts. He moaned under the continuing caresses of her gifted fingers, his lips and tongue finding their way home to nipples taut with desire.

"I don't think I can wait until Monday." He lifted his head, a grin formed on his lips. "Why don't you propose to me right now?"

"Me?" Vikki's fingertips drew provocative little squiggles across his stomach. Her chin tilted downward; her eyes formed their famous Vixen slant. In his ear she hummed the opening theme song from *Always Tomorrow*, and when she spoke her voice sounded like an announcer's. "Will Victoria propose to Dan? Will Dan propose to Victoria? For the answers to these and other questions, tune in tomorrow . . ." Her recitation was interrupted by his lips.